LEGO

DC UNIVERSE™

SUPER HEROES

BATMAN™ ULTIMATE STICKER COLLECTION

HOW TO USE THIS BOOK

Read the captions, then find the sticker that best fits in the space. (Hint: check the sticker labels for clues!)

•

Don't forget that your stickers can be stuck down and peeled off again.

•

There are lots of fantastic extra stickers too!

DK

LONDON, NEW YORK,
MELBOURNE, MUNICH, AND DELHI

Written and edited by Emma Grange
Inside pages designed by Sandra Perry
Cover designed by Jon Hall and Lisa Sodeau

First published in the United States in 2012
by DK Publishing
345 Hudson Street, New York,
New York 10014

10 9 8 7 6 5 4
005—185651—Sep/12

DORL28013

Batman created by Bob Kane

A catalog record for this book is available from the Library of Congress.

ISBN: 978-0-7566-9817-1

Color reproduction by Media Development Printing Ltd UK
Printed and bound in China by Leo Paper Products

Discover more at
www.dk.com
www.LEGO.com
www.warnerbros.com

THE DARK KNIGHT

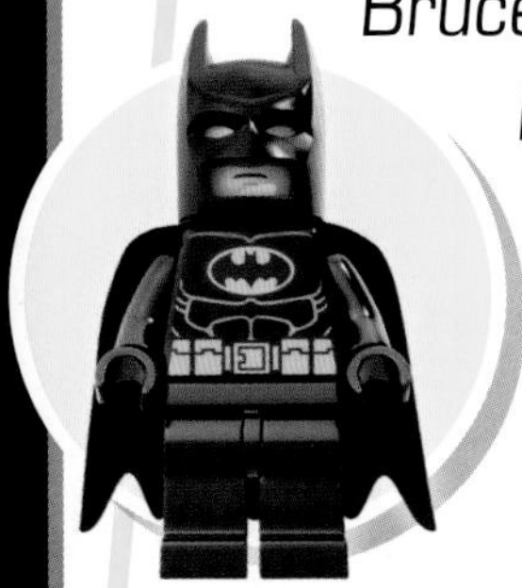

Bruce Wayne is Batman—a super hero fighting to protect his home, Gotham City, from evil! He wears a cape and cowl for protection from his enemies and to hide his secret identity. Mostly he prefers black, but sometimes he wears gray or even blue. Which of the following Batsuits is your favorite?

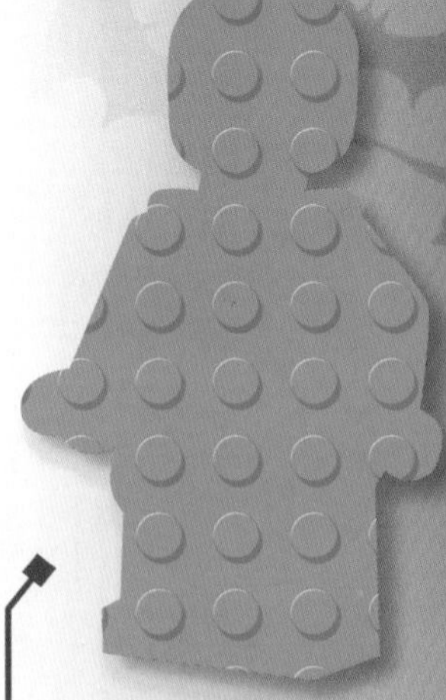

Bruce Wayne

The man behind Batman's mask is Bruce Wayne, a billionaire who works at his family company, Wayne Enterprises. Nobody suspects his secret identity!

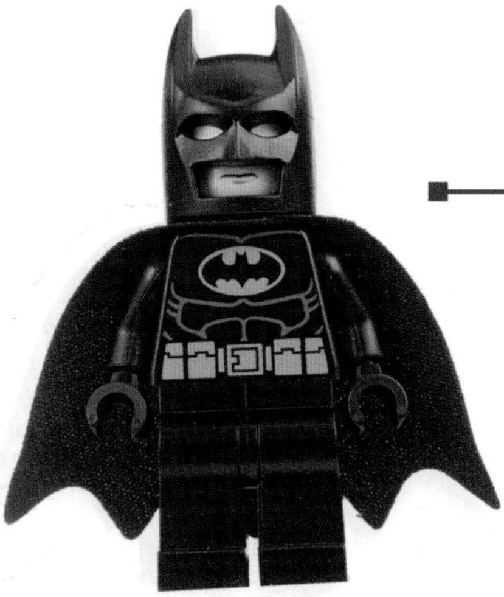

The Man in Black

Batman cloaks himself in black to hide in the dark shadowy streets of Gotham. The dark colors act as camouflage, especially at night.

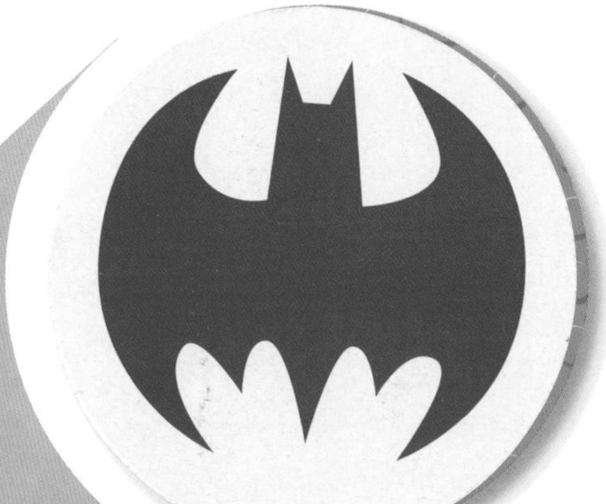

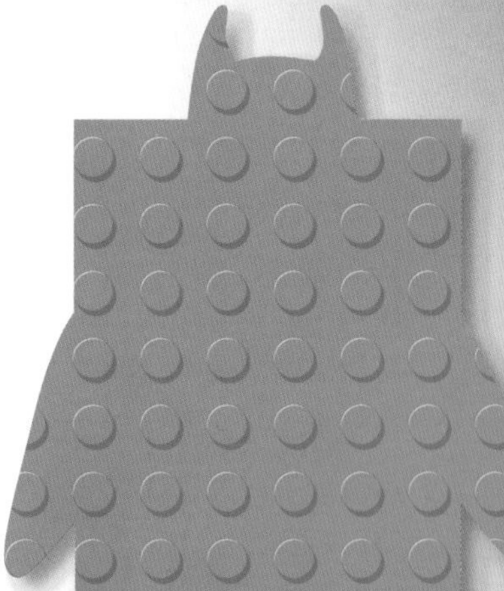

Bat-symbol

When he was young, Bruce Wayne was scared of bats. Now, as Batman, he uses this symbol of the bat to scare others!

Detective

Batman takes his crime-fighting role very seriously, and is committed to ridding the streets of rogues. He isn't known as the World's Greatest Detective for nothing!

Ready for Battle

Batman is always ready for battle. His Batsuit is fully armored and equipped with a Utility Belt for storing useful gadgets and weapons.

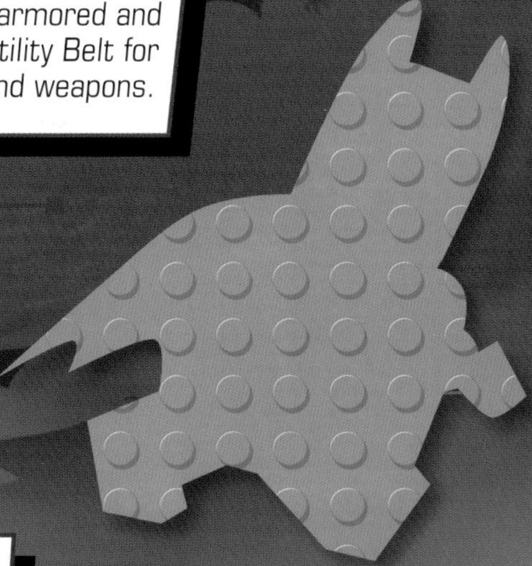

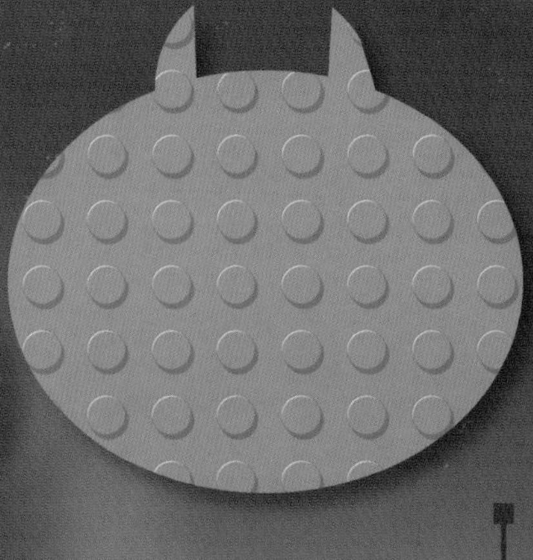

Joking Around

Batman's life isn't all doom and gloom. He often enjoys a joke and a laugh to lighten the mood down in the Batcave.

Feeling Blue

Batman also wears this blue and gray Batsuit. His blue cape can act like a parachute and is also made from strong, bullet-resistant material.

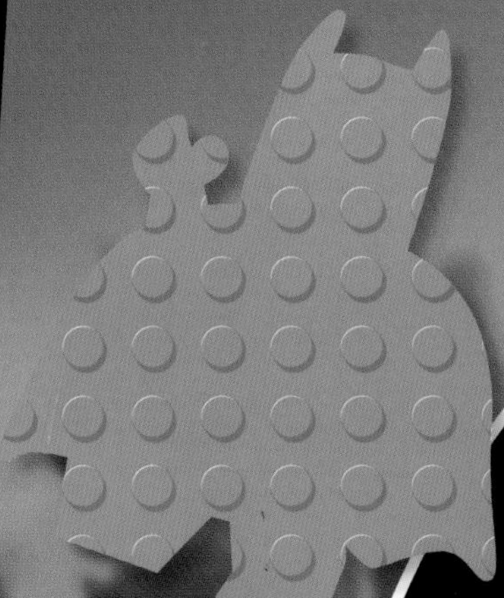

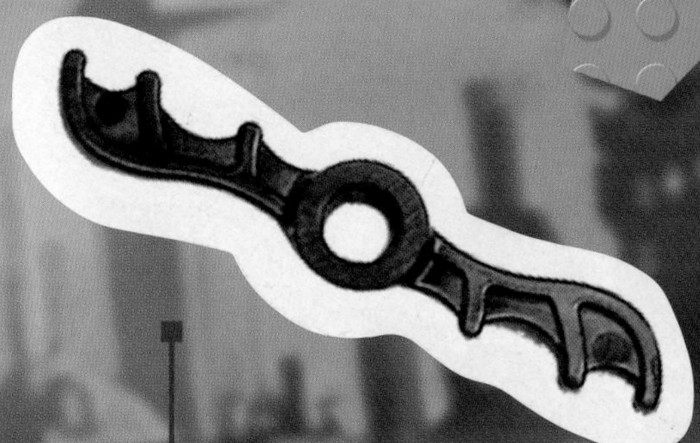

Batarangs

Batman throws these personalized weapons called Batarangs. Batarangs are based on boomerangs, with a sharp bat-shaped edge.

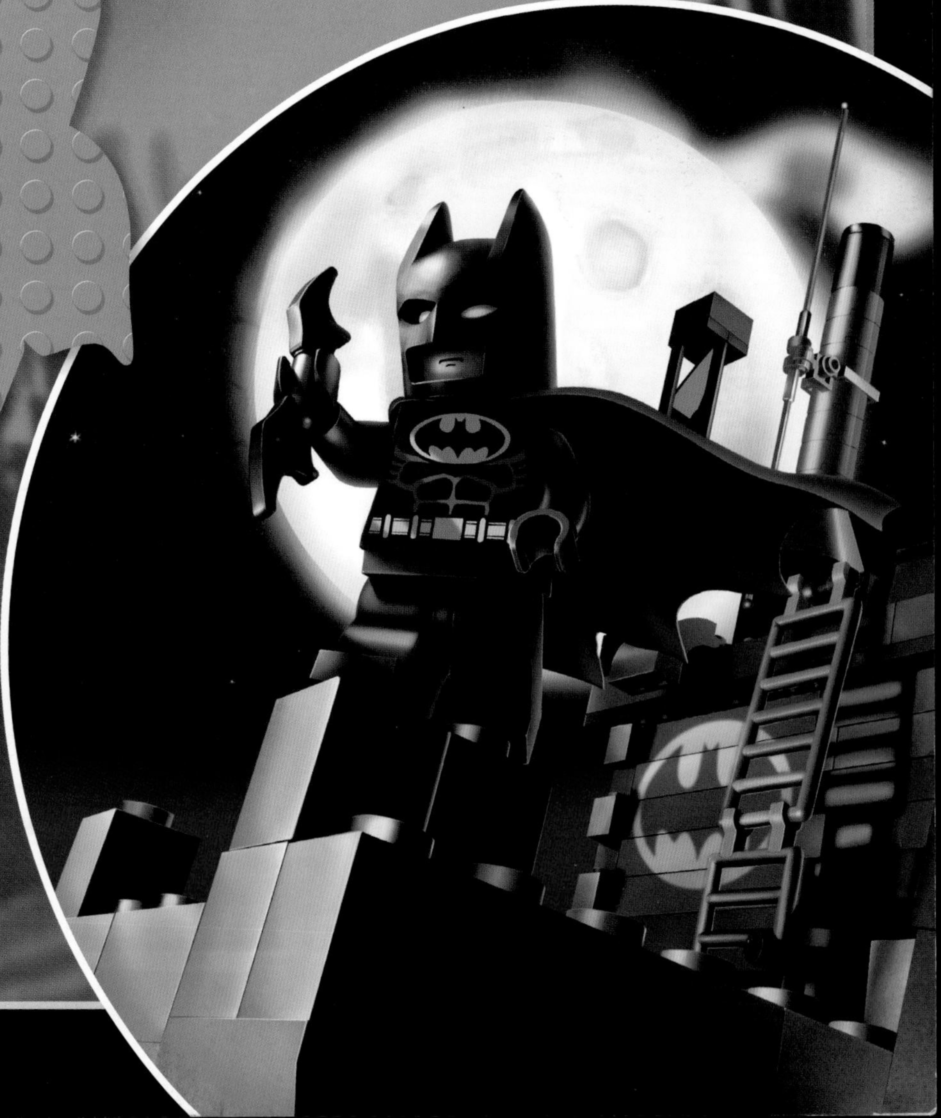

THE BATCAVE

Deep beneath the grounds of Wayne Manor, Bruce Wayne's family home, is hidden the Batcave—the secret headquarters for all things Batman. This is where the Dark Knight stores all of his equipment and is the only place he can really be himself. The cave is highly protected—at the flick of a switch, Batman can fire nets or missiles at any unwanted intruders.

Transformation Chamber

Now you see him, now you don't! Bruce steps into his transformation chamber as the smartly dressed Bruce Wayne, but steps out as the battle-ready Batman.

Batcomputer

From here, Batman can control all of his vehicles, analyze evidence from crime scenes, and even track Gotham's most wanted.

ALERT!

Service, Please!

Batman often works very long hours down in the Batcave, so he relies upon his butler Alfred to bring him refreshments.

Locked Up

In the event of an invasion, the Batcave features a holding cell for locking up foes. Poison Ivy has been caught in the act and does not look pleased...

Welcome to the Batcave! Use your extra stickers to create your own scene...

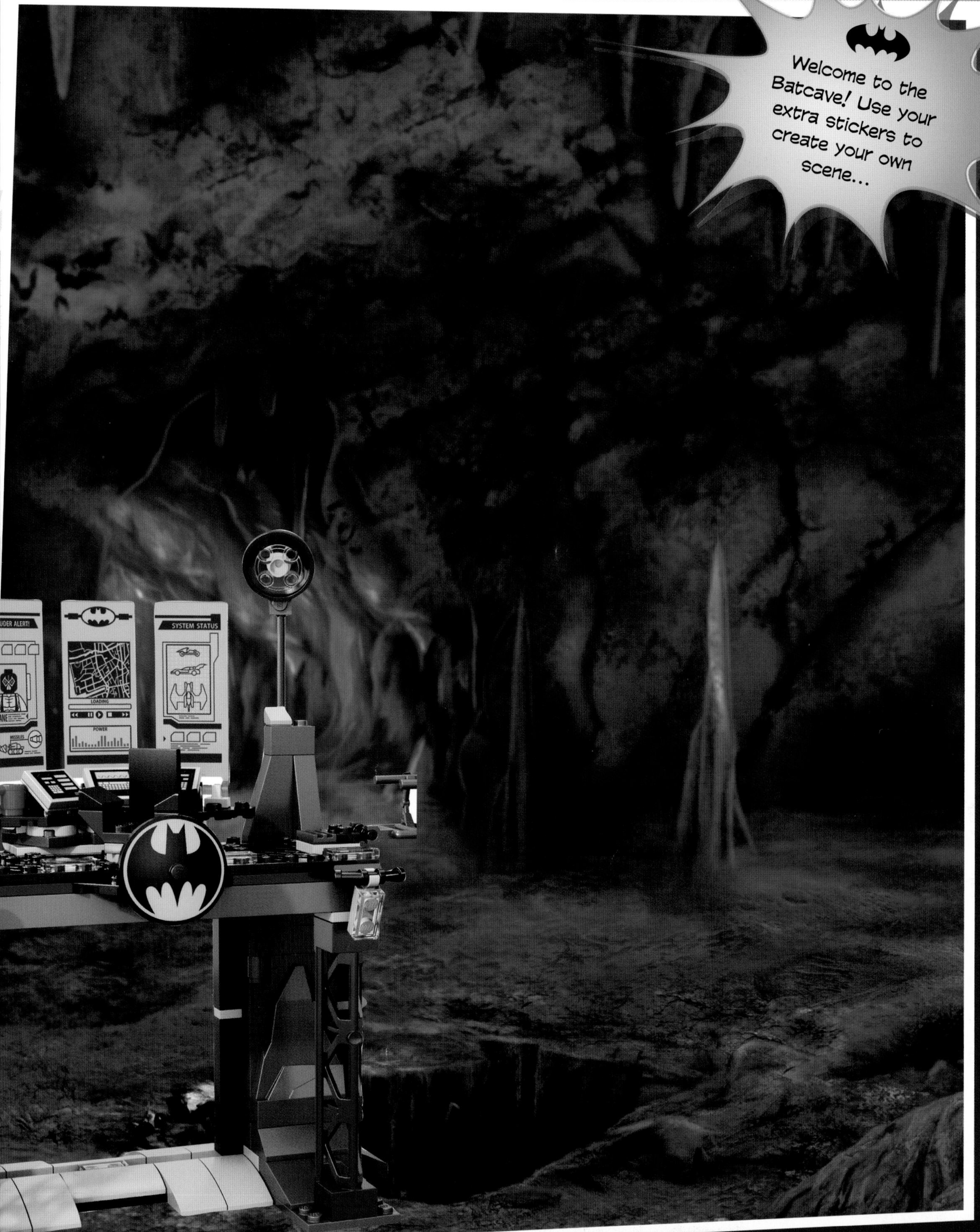
SYSTEM STATUS
LOADING
POWER

BAT-VEHICLES

Batman has a whole convoy of cars, cycles, and other vehicles for racing around Gotham City. All of them are equipped with the most hi-tech gadgets and weapons available so that the Caped Crusader can counter any attack launched against him. With Batman in the driver's seat, the criminals of Gotham don't stand a chance!

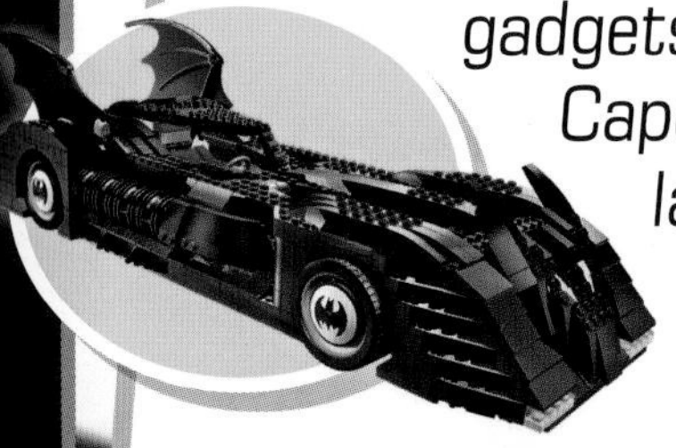

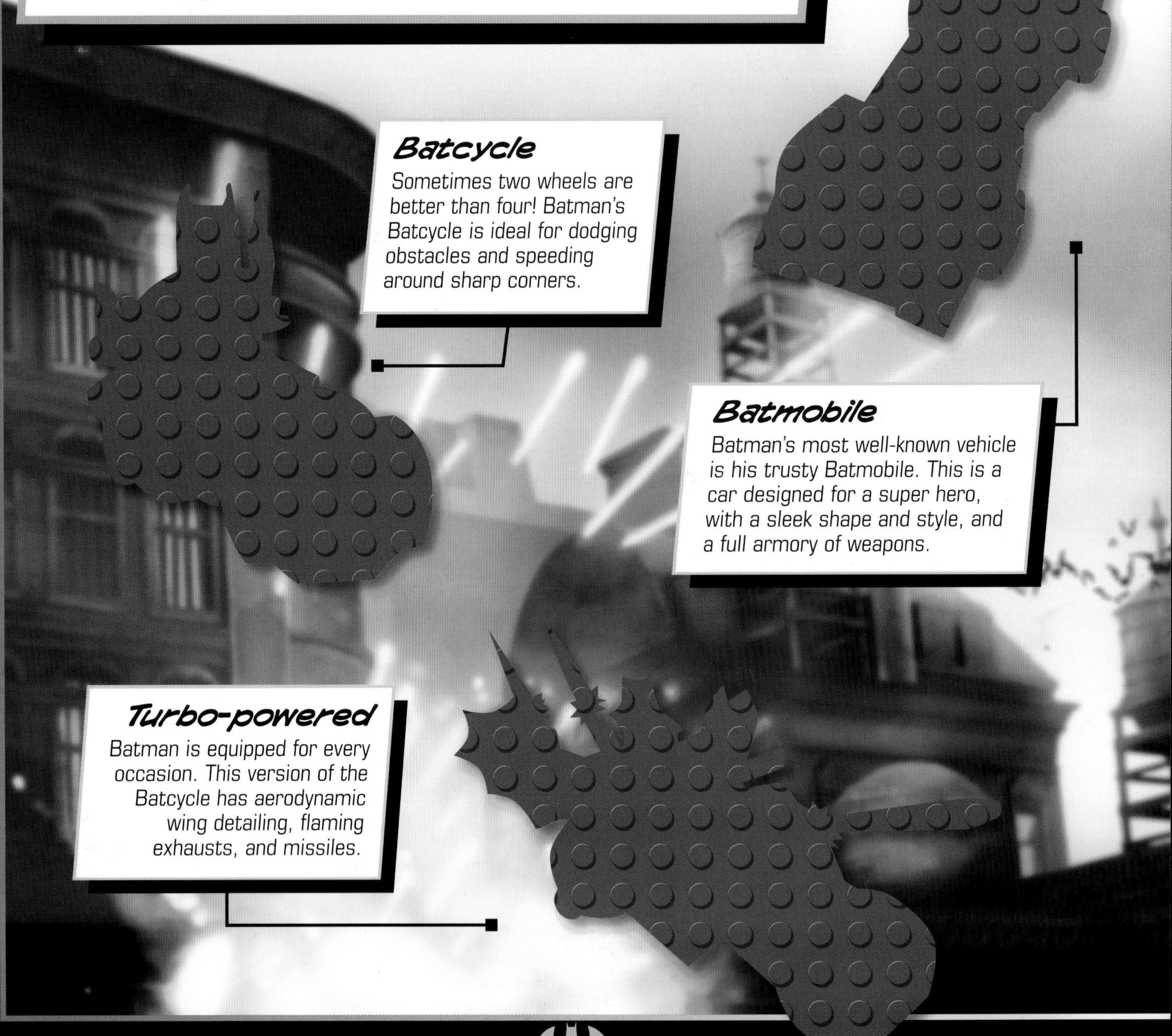

Batcycle

Sometimes two wheels are better than four! Batman's Batcycle is ideal for dodging obstacles and speeding around sharp corners.

Batmobile

Batman's most well-known vehicle is his trusty Batmobile. This is a car designed for a super hero, with a sleek shape and style, and a full armory of weapons.

Turbo-powered

Batman is equipped for every occasion. This version of the Batcycle has aerodynamic wing detailing, flaming exhausts, and missiles.

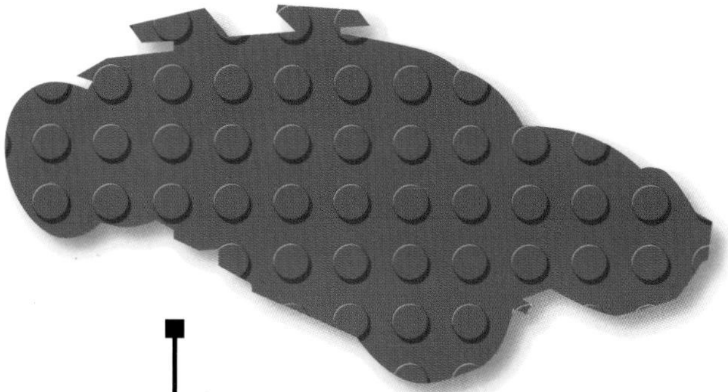

Batblade

This vehicle is still under development in the Batcave, but when finished it will tackle icy and snowy landscapes with ease. Mr. Freeze be warned!

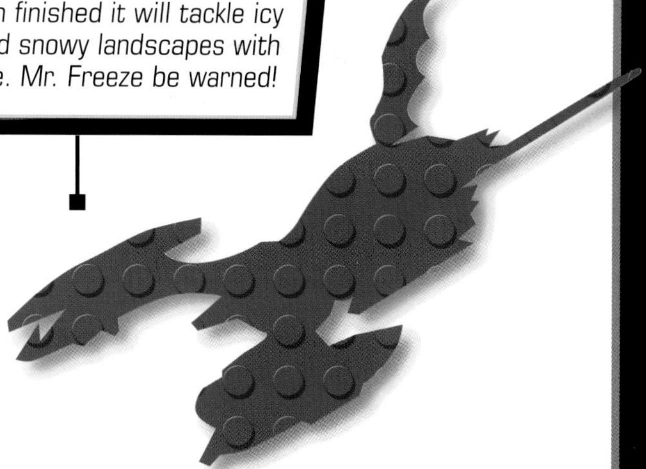

The Tumbler

The Tumbler is a truly terrifying prospect. Fully armored from top to bottom, this machine will flatten anything in its path.

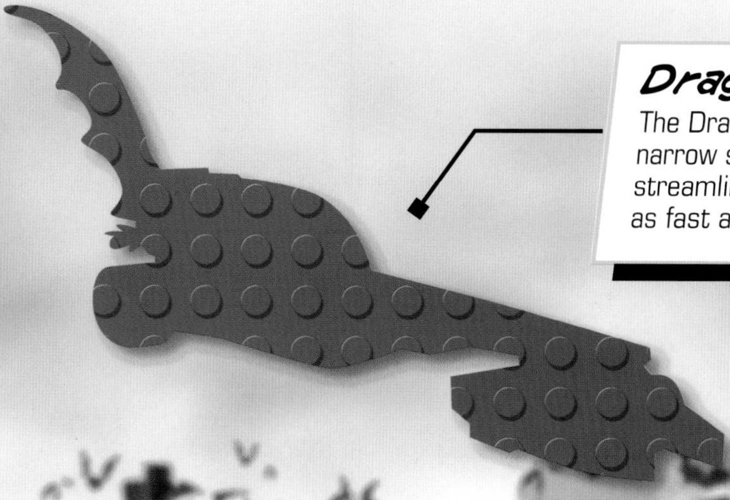

Dragster

The Dragster is ideal for Gotham's narrow streets. The Dragster is streamlined for speed, and is just as fast as the Batmobile.

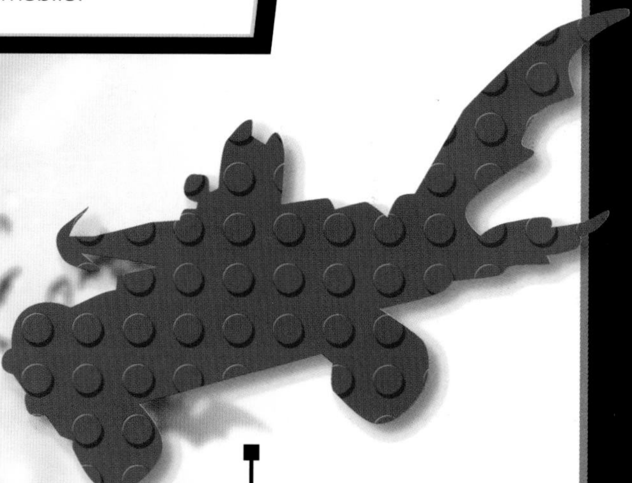

Bat-Tank

When Batman needs to venture off-road, his Bat-Tank—with its powerful caterpillar tracks—is the perfect vehicle for the job.

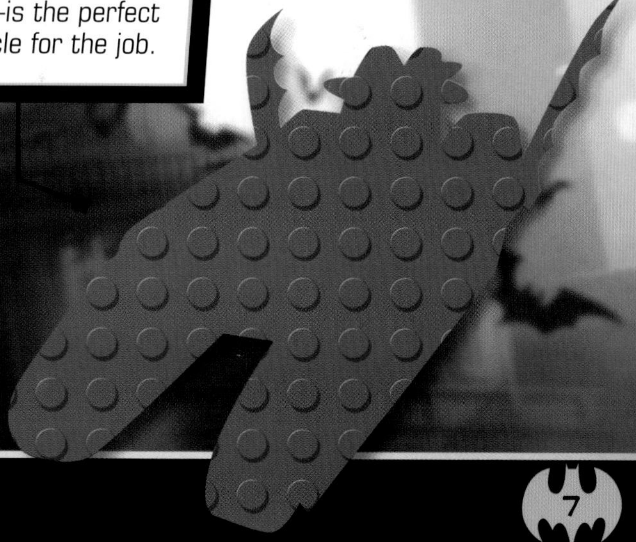

Batman's Buggy

Gotham's criminals may try to escape, but Batman is never far behind, and he can reel them back in with the harpoon on his buggy.

ROGUES GALLERY

The Caped Crusader has attracted a lot of attention in his fight against crime. Many colorful characters have emerged to try their luck against Batman and they all have their own agenda. Some want the Dark Knight defeated so that they can continue their criminal ways without interruption, others just want to outwit the World's Greatest Detective!

Two-Face

Harvey Dent used to be a lawyer working for Gotham City. Now he lives a double life as Two-Face, sometimes acting for good, sometimes for evil.

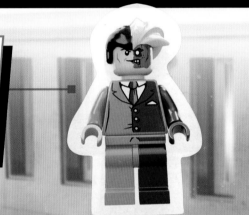

The Joker

The Joker is Batman's constant nemesis. With his crazed clownish grin and his love of causing chaos, the Joker is always unpredictable.

The Riddler

Edward Nigma loves riddles and puzzles. He especially loves setting seemingly impossible traps for Batman in the hope that he'll trip up.

Catwoman

Selina Kyle is Catwoman—a complicated cat-like character. Sometimes she and Batman work together, and sometimes they fight tooth and claw.

The Scarecrow

Dr. Jonathan Crane was once a psychology professor, but he descended into madness. Under the alias Scarecrow, he is now a professional criminal, frightening citizens for fun.

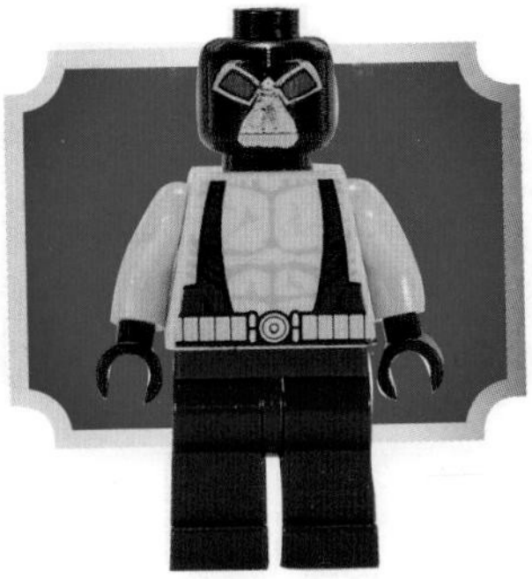

Bane

Bane looks brutish, but his super-strength is matched with super-intelligence. Of all of Batman's foes, Bane is one of the most dangerous.

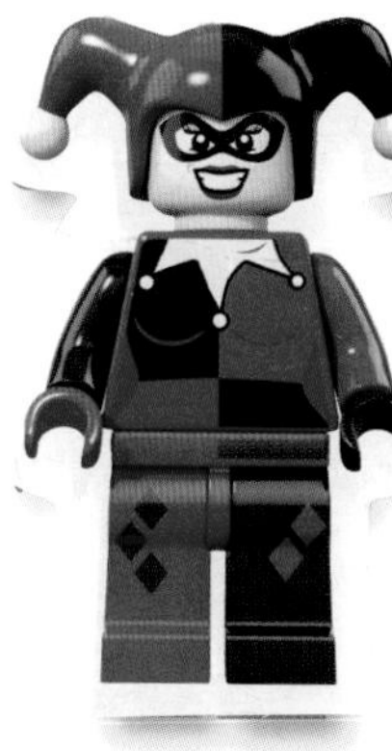

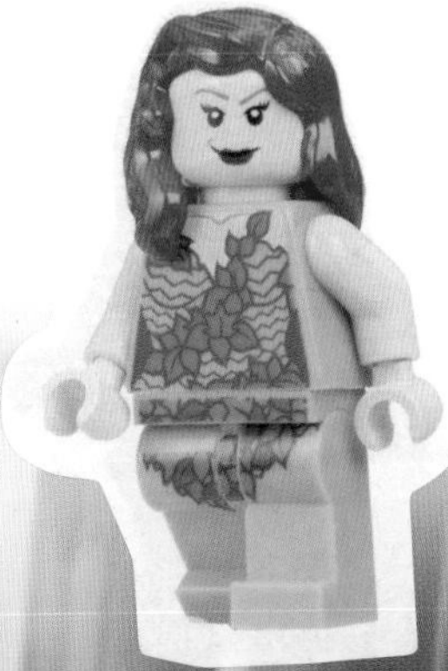

Poison Ivy

Pamela Isley developed a toxic touch. She has the ability to control plants and can use them to manipulate people. Batman knows Poison Ivy cannot be trusted.

Harley Quinn

Harley Quinn might look fun, but her costume masks a cruel heart. Her love for the Joker means she'll attack anyone who tries to get in his way.

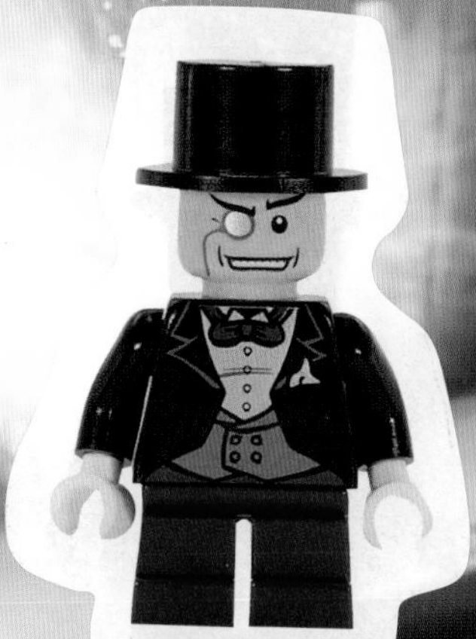

Mr. Freeze

Victor Fries depends on sub-zero temperatures to survive after a tragic lab accident. Now he likes to freeze anyone who crosses him.

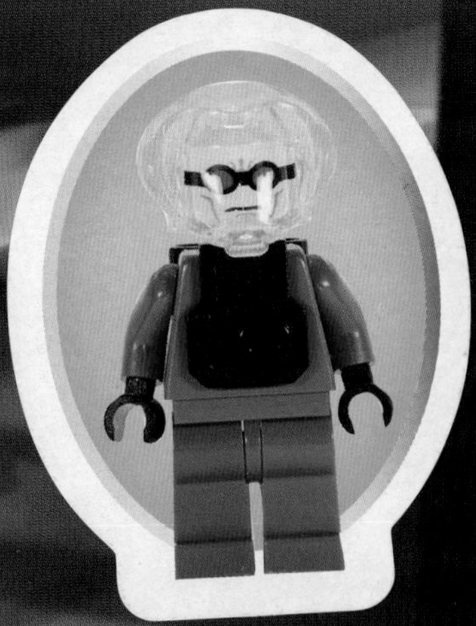

The Penguin

Oswald Cobblepot made up for his small stature by becoming the bird-obsessed, wealthy crime lord known as the Penguin.

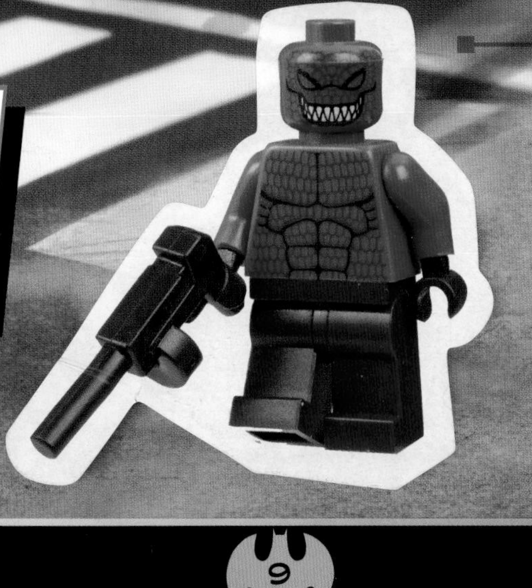

Killer Croc

From his glaring red eyes and scaly green skin, it is clear that Killer Croc is one vicious criminal! Like many others, he's after Batman…

GOTHAM CITY

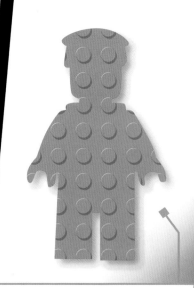

Bruce Wayne knows more than anyone how dangerous Gotham City can be. At a young age, he watched a criminal shoot his parents in a street called Crime Alley. From that moment he vowed to rid his city of all evil, and thus Batman was born! Here are some of the places on the Caped Crusader's patrol route...

At the Bank

Gotham City's bank is regularly targeted by robbers. Two-Face is one rogue who has more than once tried to make off with a stolen bank safe.

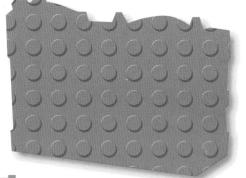

Bank Guard

Working at the bank is a tough job. This security guard must protect the vaults of valuables, while maintaining a cheerful smile for customers.

Arkham Asylum

Arkham Asylum is a hospital for the criminally insane. Unfortunately most of Gotham's felons are crazy, so Arkham is nearly always full!

Patients' Ward

There are many rooms in Arkham Asylum. One is for treating and interrogating patients in the hope that they can be released back into society.

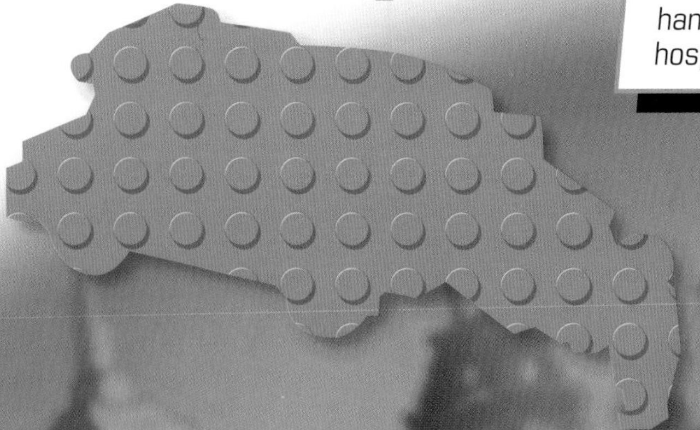

Carried Away

Sometimes the patients at Arkham have to be transported elsewhere. An ambulance is on hand to take patients to other hospitals—or prison!

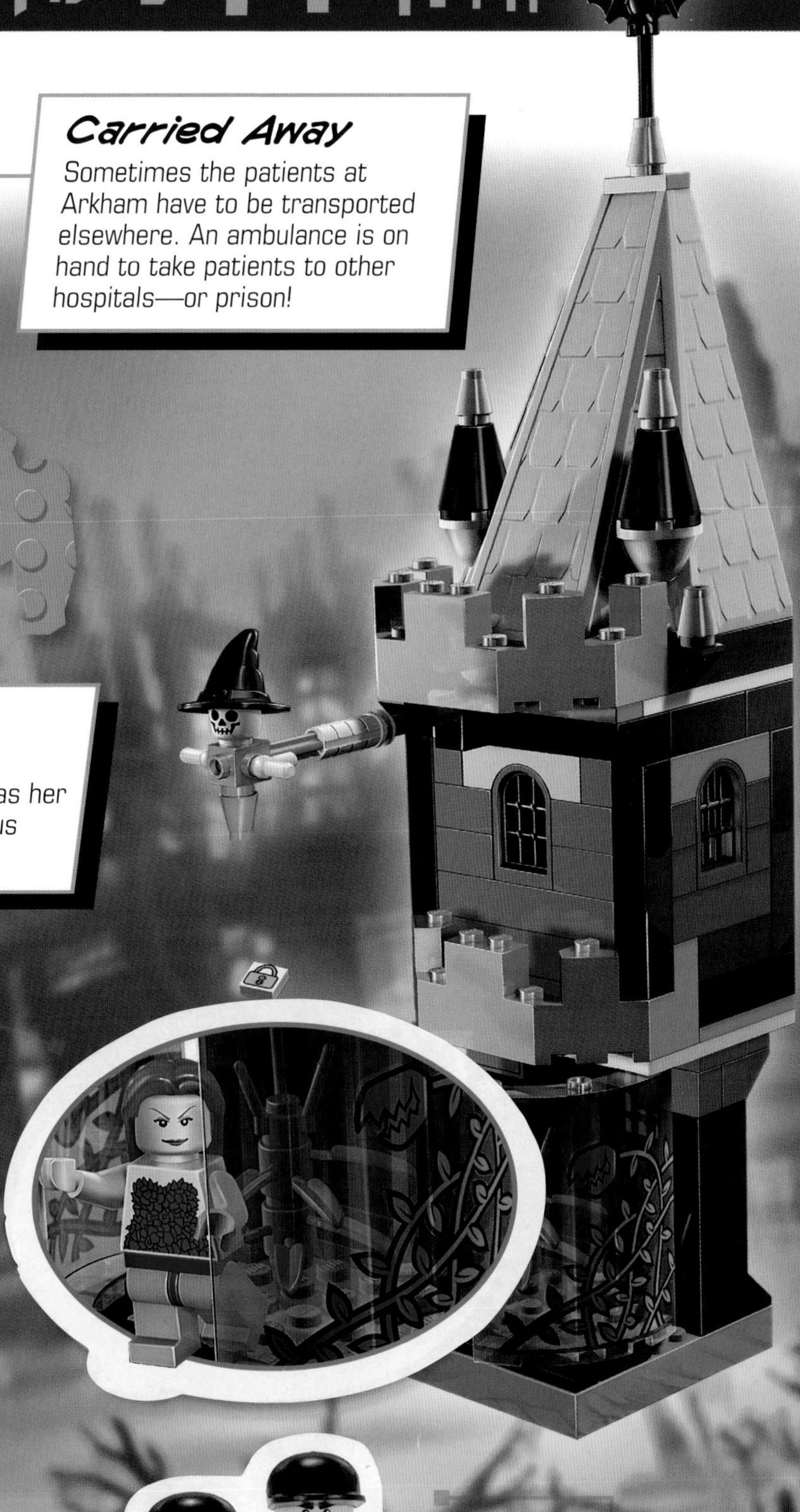

Ivy's Tower

Poison Ivy is almost a permanent resident in Arkham Asylum. She has her own tower, furnished with poisonous plants to make her feel at home.

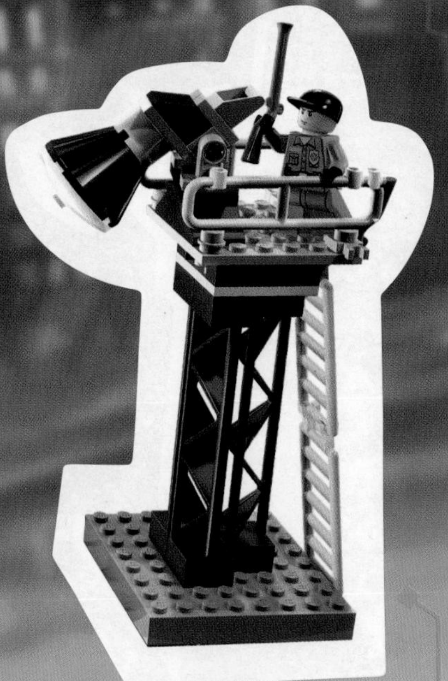

Keeping Watch

The inmates at Arkham Asylum often try to escape, so the guards must keep a constant watch on the perimeter.

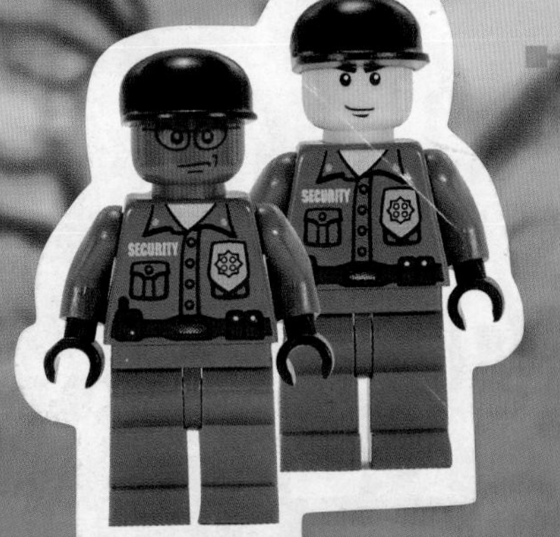

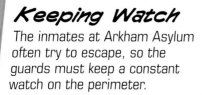

Asylum Guards

The guards at Arkham Asylum have to be stern. Their charges are well known for staging breakouts...

FAITHFUL FRIENDS

Batman isn't alone in his fight to protect Gotham City. Over the years he has built up a small but loyal group of friends and allies that are as close to him as family. Batman knows he can always rely on the help of his crime-fighting partner, Robin, or his butler Alfred, to get him out of a tight spot.

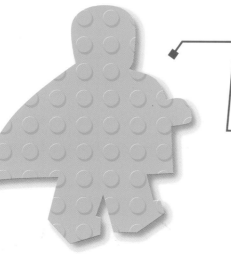

Robin

Tim Drake became Batman's partner when he discovered Batman's secret identity. Now he is a most trusted member of Batman's circle.

Alfred

Alfred Pennyworth is more than just a butler. He is also a father figure to the orphaned Bruce and helps to keep his identity as Batman a secret.

Teen Wonder

The Teen Wonder has grown up under Batman's teaching. He is now ready to tackle crime-fighting adventures of his own.

Nightwing

Dick Grayson was the first Robin. Now he continues to help Batman fight crime as Nightwing, racing to his next mission on his unique motorcycle.

Redbird

Robin's scuba jet is known as the Redbird. It is colored in the same red, green, and yellow colors as Robin's circus-inspired costume.

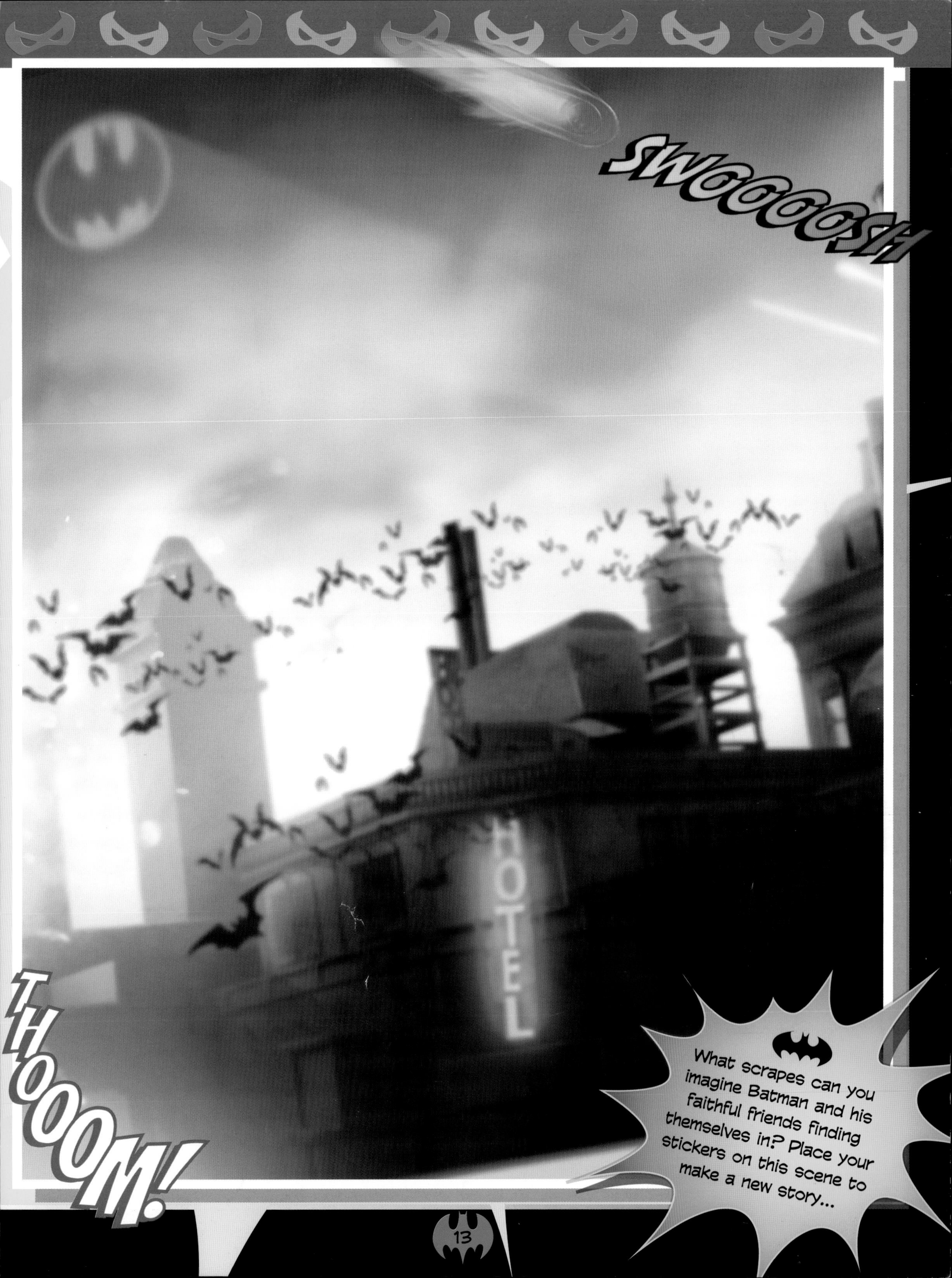
SWOOOOSH
HOTEL
THOOOM!
What scrapes can you imagine Batman and his faithful friends finding themselves in? Place your stickers on this scene to make a new story...

THE JOKER

Meet Batman's archenemy: the Joker. This clownish character used to be the low-life criminal Red Hood, until a freak accident with a vat of acid dyed his hair bright green and his skin white. Taking on the persona of a clown, the Joker brings a touch of craziness to all of his attempts to beat Batman.

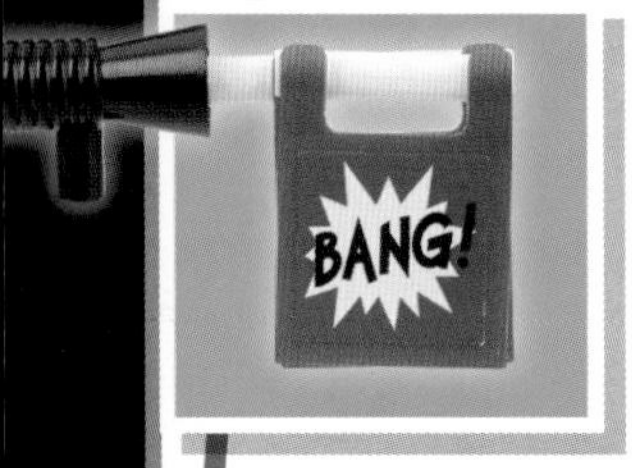
BANG!

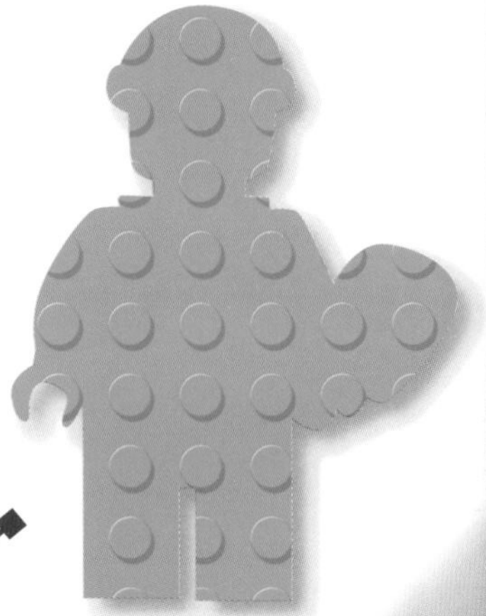

Venomous

Don't let this henchman tempt you—these popsicles are flavored with the Joker's homemade poison, Joker Venom.

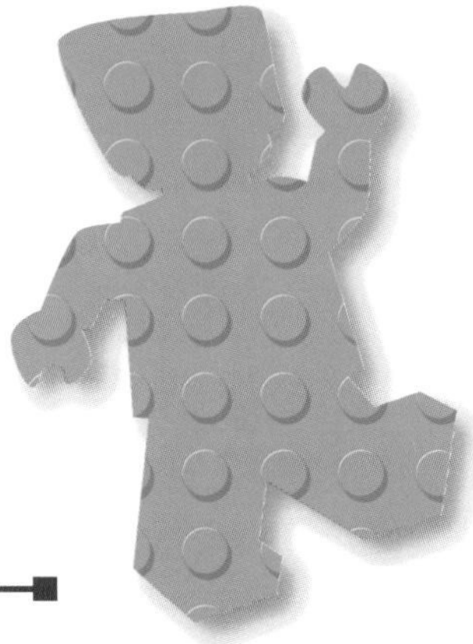

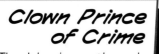

Clown Prince of Crime

The Joker is mostly mad. His face is fixed with a permanent grin and he is instantly recognizable by his bright clothes.

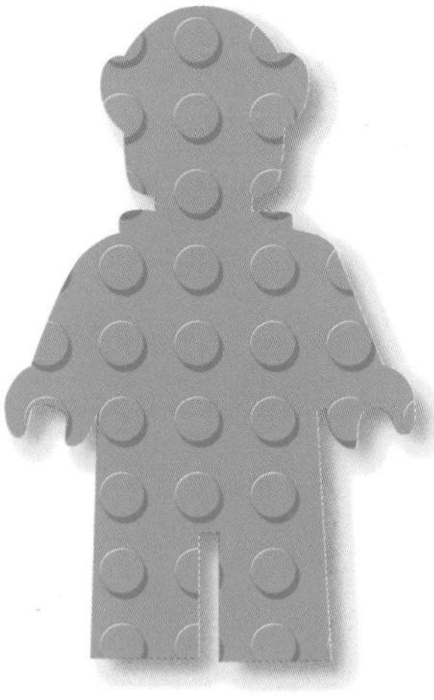

Clowning Around

This goon wears makeup and an outfit similar to his master's. Working for the Joker isn't much fun—hence the firm frown on his face.

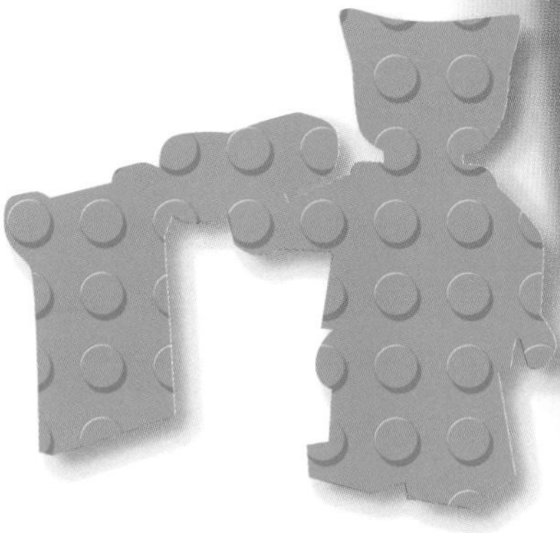

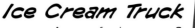

"Bang!"

Always with a love for the theatrical, the Joker has a personalized gun that reads, "Bang!" to alarm his enemies. What a joker!

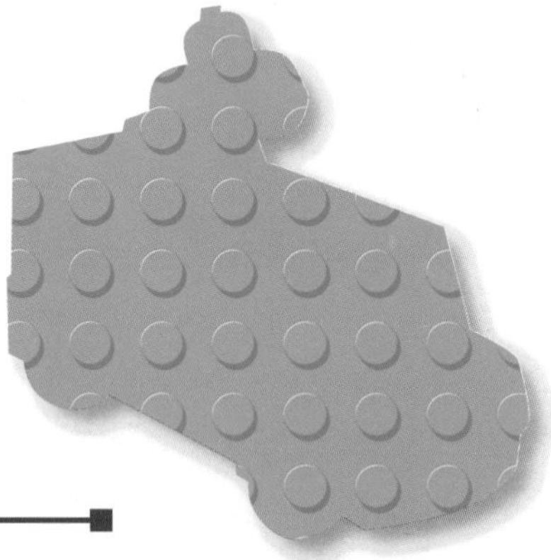

Ice Cream Truck

Anyone for ice cream? The Joker's Ice Cream Truck looks innocent but holds sinister surprises in the form of hidden missiles, a cannon, and other weapons.

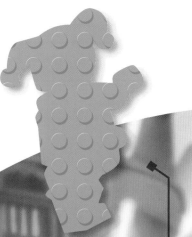

Flying High

The Joker has an unusual method of getting around. While flying high in his Joker Copter he hangs from its ladder to get a better shot at his targets.

Harlequin

The Joker's girlfriend, Harley Quinn, has followed the Joker's example: she too dresses in a comically bright costume—that of a jester, or harlequin.

The Joke Card

The Joker likes people to know which atrocious acts he is responsible for, so he often leaves a Joker card at the scene of the crime.

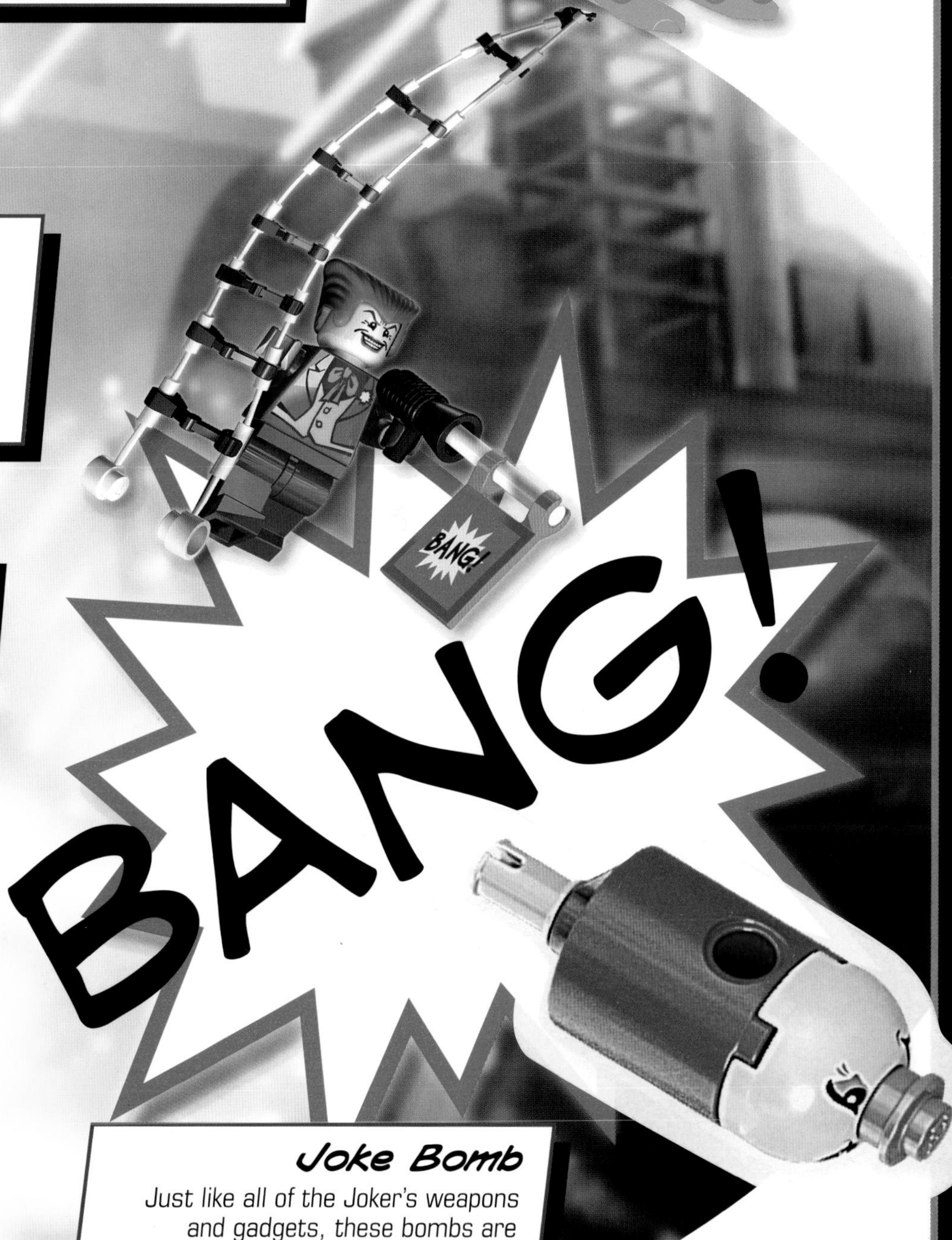
BANG!
BANG!

Joke Bomb

Just like all of the Joker's weapons and gadgets, these bombs are designed to look clownish and fun, while causing chaos and destruction.

THE PENGUIN & MR. FREEZE

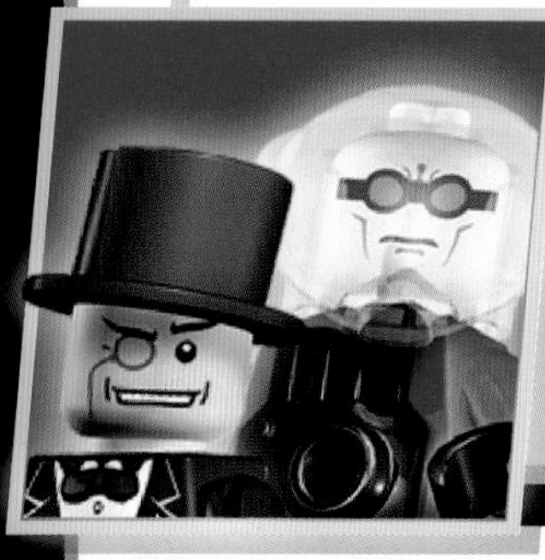

Villains the Penguin and Mr. Freeze may have their differences, but they have one thing in common: they both hate Batman for foiling their plans. Now they want revenge! Together they have united to defeat him once and for all. Will this mean a chilly end for the Dark Knight?

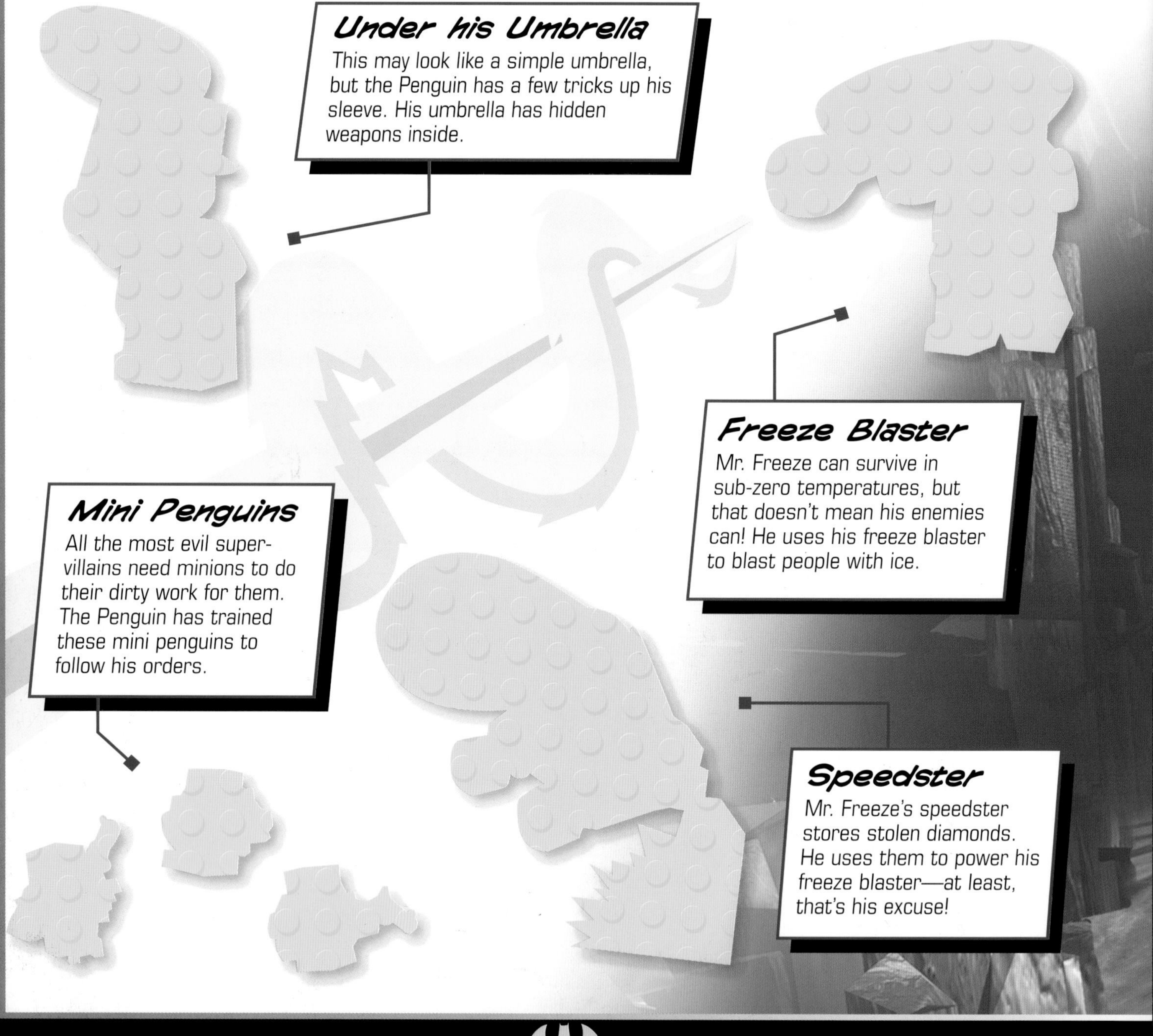

Under his Umbrella

This may look like a simple umbrella, but the Penguin has a few tricks up his sleeve. His umbrella has hidden weapons inside.

Freeze Blaster

Mr. Freeze can survive in sub-zero temperatures, but that doesn't mean his enemies can! He uses his freeze blaster to blast people with ice.

Mini Penguins

All the most evil super-villains need minions to do their dirty work for them. The Penguin has trained these mini penguins to follow his orders.

Speedster

Mr. Freeze's speedster stores stolen diamonds. He uses them to power his freeze blaster—at least, that's his excuse!

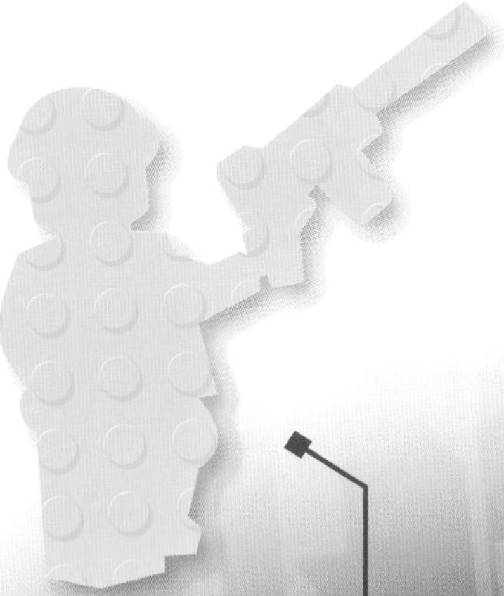

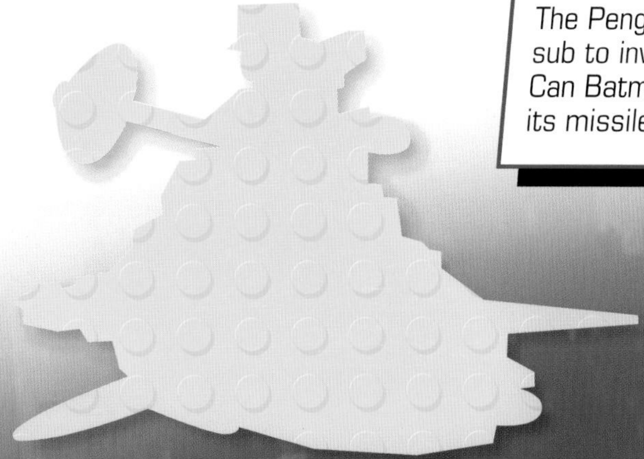

Missile-firing Sub

The Penguin uses his missile-firing sub to invade the Batcave. Can Batman and Robin dodge its missiles and rockets?

Mr. Henchman

This henchman takes orders from Mr. Freeze. He looks like he means business with his loaded guns and chilling glare.

Submarine

This submarine looks as mean as the Penguin himself. It can dive deep beneath the waves—perfect for quests to find sunken treasure.

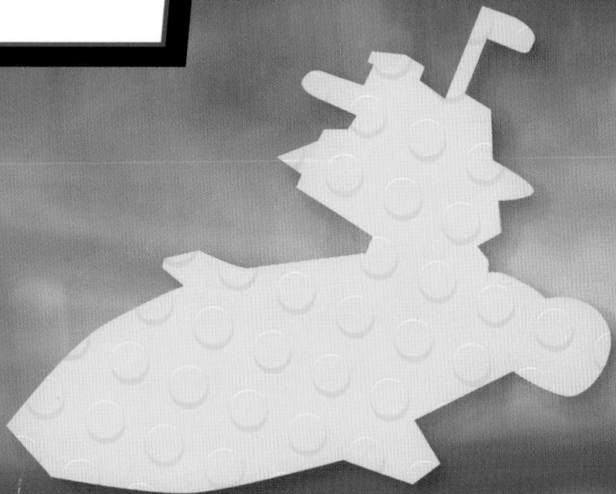

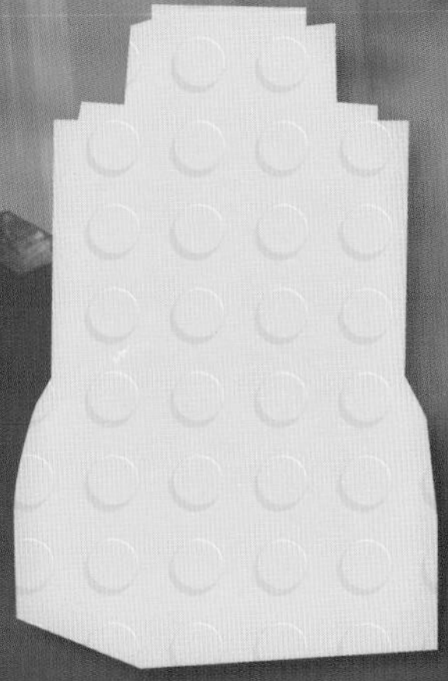

Frozen in Ice

The Penguin and Mr. Freeze have invaded the Batcave! Alfred needs some help after being blasted by Mr. Freeze's freeze ray gun.

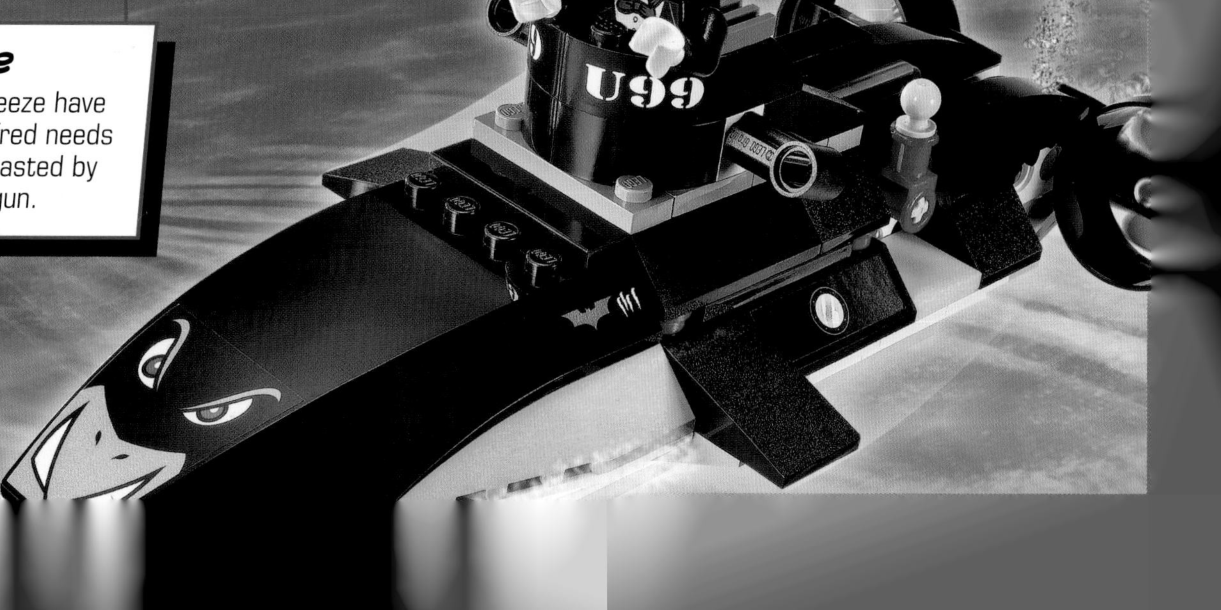
U99

ATTACK ON THE WATER

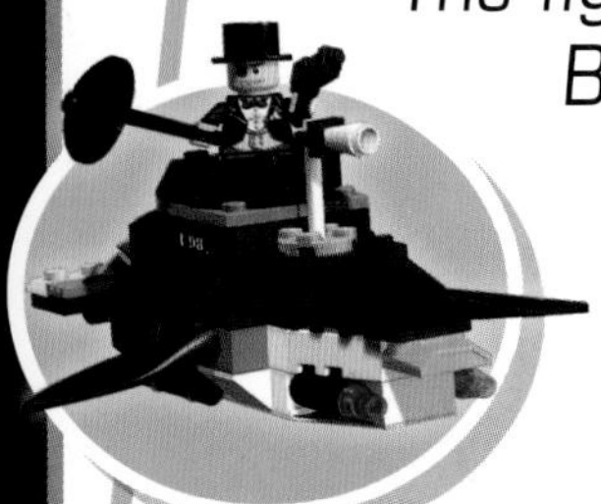

The fight for Gotham City continues on the water. Some of Batman's foes are naturally nautical, but Batman can make waves of his own with these vessels created specially for speedy sea voyages. Perhaps Killer Croc shouldn't look so confident—not with Batman and Robin hot on his tail...

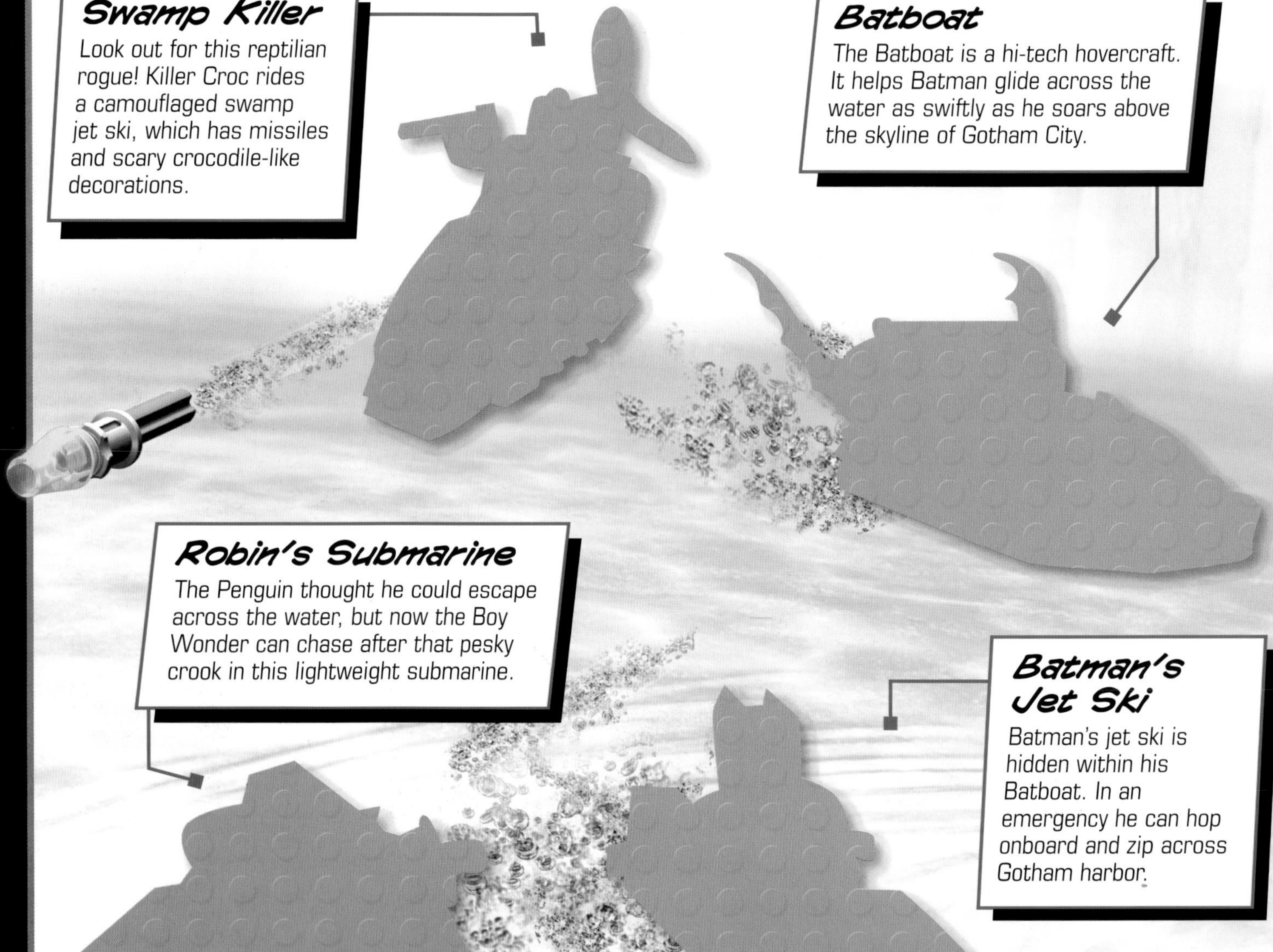

Swamp Killer

Look out for this reptilian rogue! Killer Croc rides a camouflaged swamp jet ski, which has missiles and scary crocodile-like decorations.

Batboat

The Batboat is a hi-tech hovercraft. It helps Batman glide across the water as swiftly as he soars above the skyline of Gotham City.

Robin's Submarine

The Penguin thought he could escape across the water, but now the Boy Wonder can chase after that pesky crook in this lightweight submarine.

Batman's Jet Ski

Batman's jet ski is hidden within his Batboat. In an emergency he can hop onboard and zip across Gotham harbor.

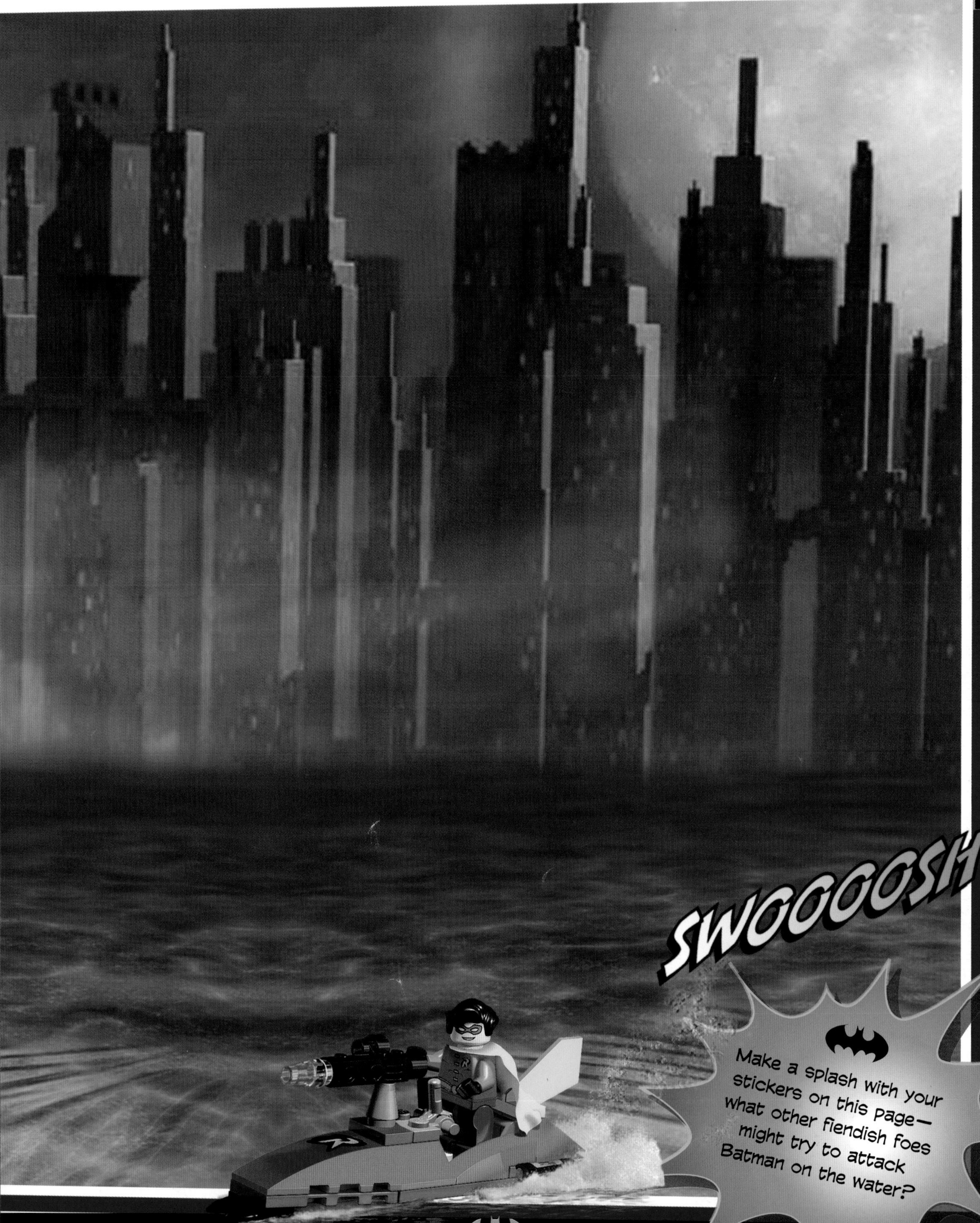
SWOOOOSH

Make a splash with your stickers on this page—what other fiendish foes might try to attack Batman on the water?

TAKE TO THE SKIES

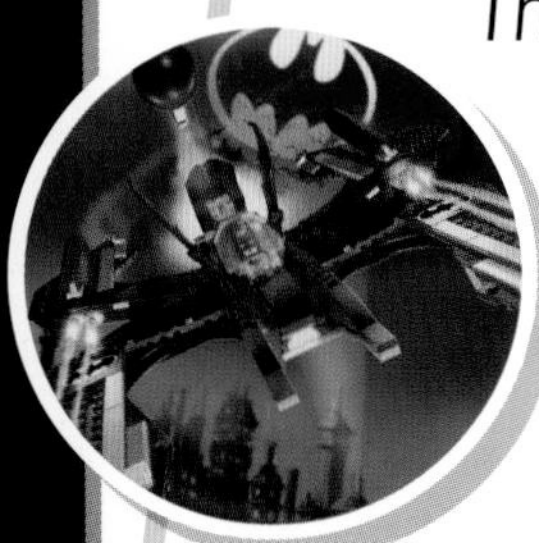

There's nothing more exciting than when Batman and his enemies engage in an air-bourne battle. The Caped Crusader isn't the only one with a fleet of fantastic vehicles. Many of Gotham's madcap criminals have their own flying machines and can take to the skies in jets and copters of all shapes and sizes...

The Batwing

Look out! Batman's supersonic jet, the Batwing, is sleek and streamlined. It is adorned with the bat-symbol and is packed with hidden weapons.

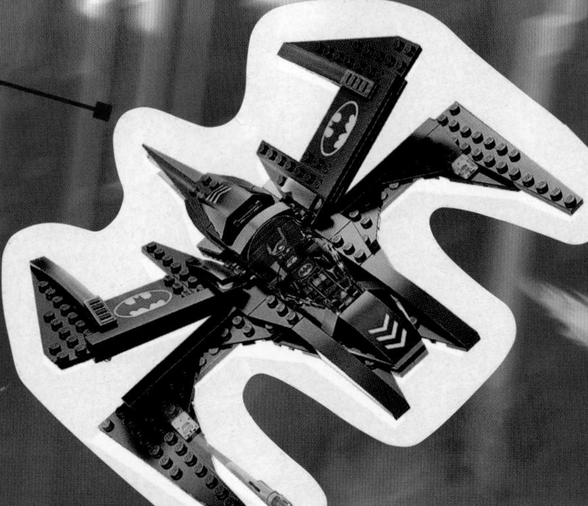

The Joker Copter

The Joker has brought his usual brand of madness to his personalized helicopter. The Joker Copter is armed with lots of wacky weaponry, including Venom bombs.

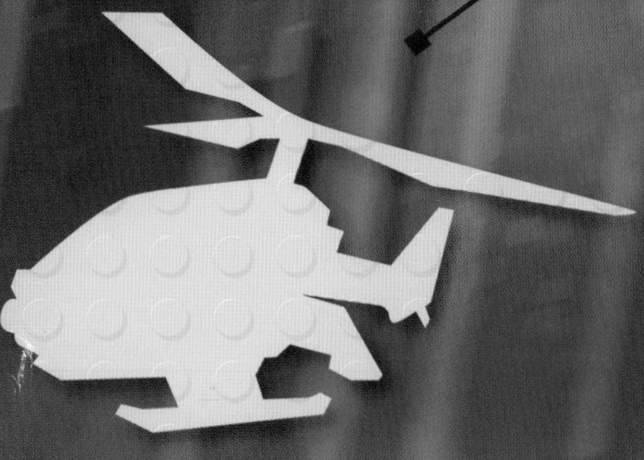

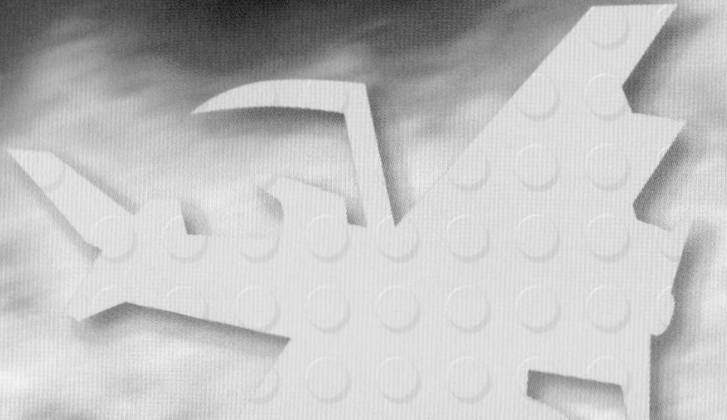

Biplane

The Scarecrow's biplane may look old fashioned, but it is perfect for carrying all of the bombs he wants to drop on Gotham City.

Batcopter

The sound of the Batcopter approaching strikes fear into the hearts of the Dark Knight's enemies! Its powerful rotor transports Batman to any emergency in a hurry.

Bat-Glider

The Bat-Glider has wings shaped like a bat's and is steered with a simple turn of its handle. Its design allows Batman to drop down on villains silently.

Jetpack

The Riddler has invented a clever way to soar out of Batman's reach with this jetpack. Up, up, and away!

SWOOOOSH

Flying Batman

Batman can't really fly, but with these aerodynamic wings strapped to his jetpack, he can swoop over Gotham just like a real bat.

Gas Bombs

The Scarecrow wants to infect Gotham City with fear. These bombs contain a gas that causes terror. And they look terrifying too!

VILLAINS' VEHICLES

Batman may have some of the most advanced transportation the world has ever seen, but his enemies also have some cool and crazy cars. They can go just as far and just as fast as Batman, and they have just as many weapons. These vehicles are as vicious as the villains driving them...

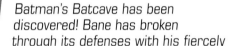

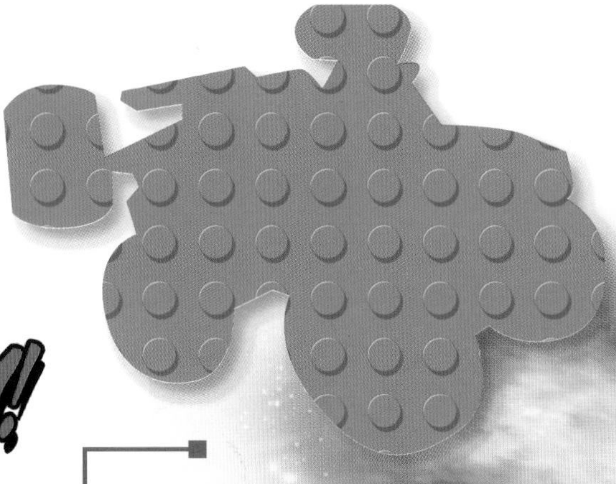

VROOOM!

Spinning Drill Tank

Batman's Batcave has been discovered! Bane has broken through its defenses with his fiercely powerful Spinning Drill Tank.

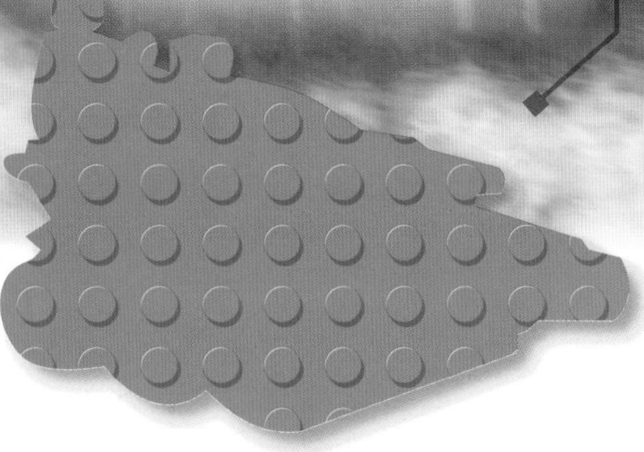

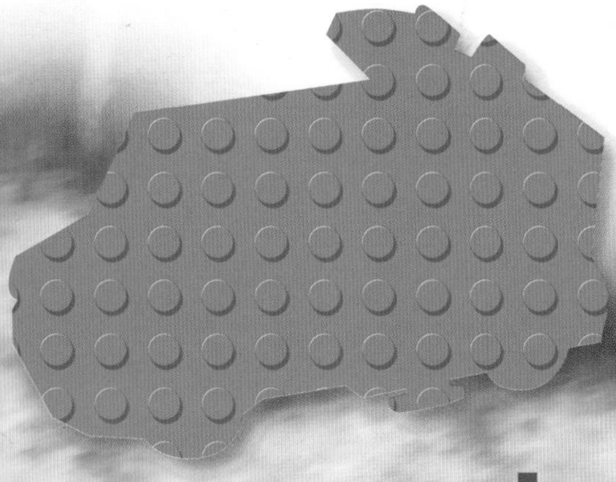

Harley's Hammer Truck

Harley Quinn climbs aboard her Monster Hammer Truck for a serious mission—she wants to "whack a bat." Batman, beware!

Bane's Bike

Bane's three-wheeled dirt bike can tackle the rockiest and muddiest of off-road terrains.

Escape Vehicle

This may look like an ordinary bank truck, but it is actually Two-Face's escape van! He plans to make off with all sorts of stolen goods...

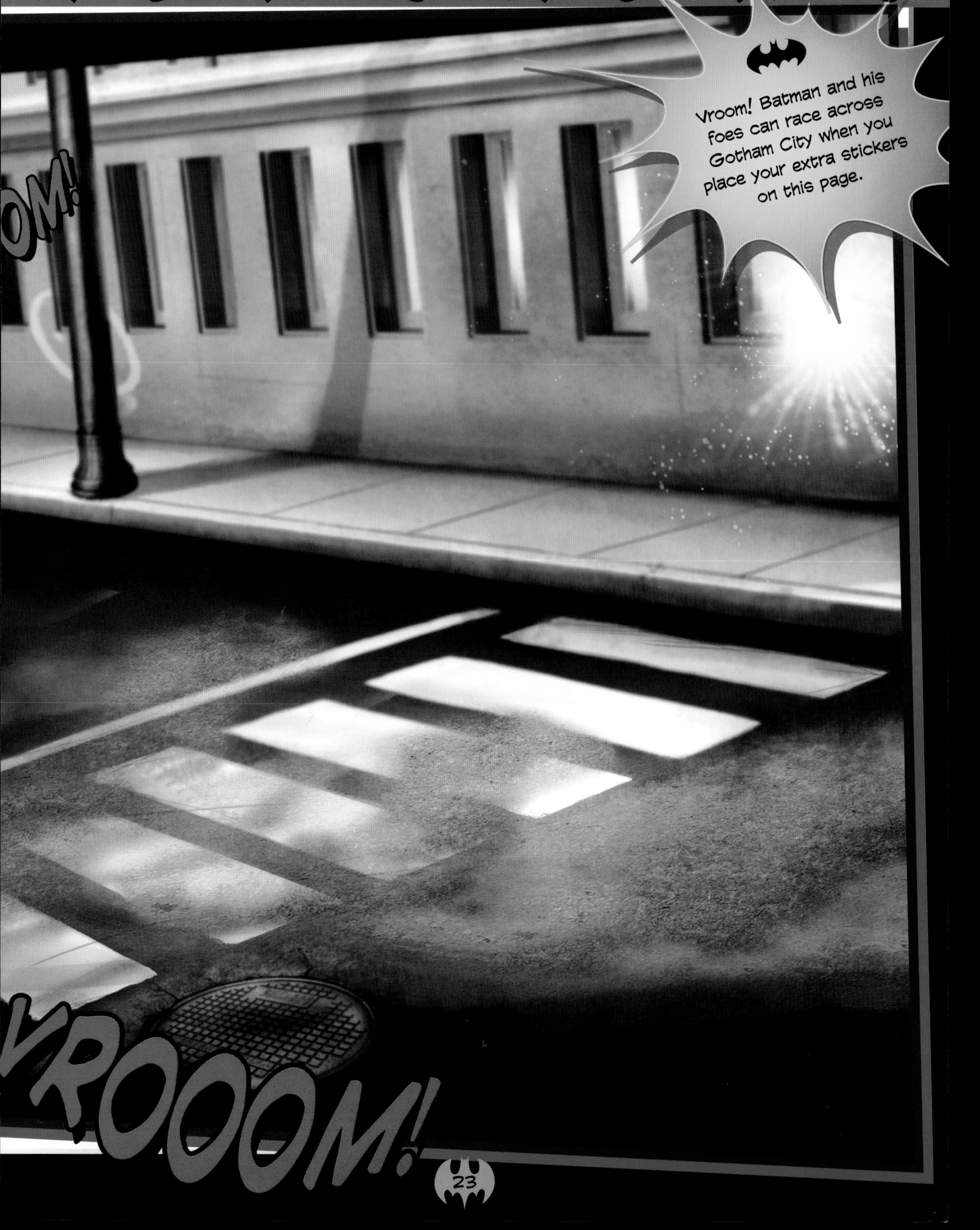
OM!
Vroom! Batman and his foes can race across Gotham City when you place your extra stickers on this page.
VROOOM!

WEAPONS & GADGETS

Batman isn't the only one with a collection of unusual and unique weapons and gadgets. Both his friends and his foes have followed his example and come armed to the teeth with a wide range of amazing devices to use during battle.

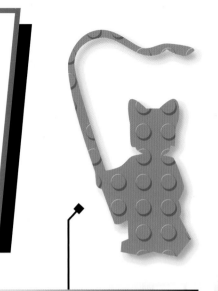

Feline Skills

Catwoman is a gifted athlete. She can match Batman blow for blow in a fight, and uses her trademark whip to fling herself across rooftops.

Harley's Hammer

Harley Quinn has a gleeful grin on her face because she's armed with a huge hammer! She is out to catch and squash a certain Caped Crusader.

Bomb Detonator

The Joker loves causing huge explosions. He plans to use this big red bomb detonator to blow up some of Gotham's tallest buildings.

The Scarecrow's Scythe

Scythes are usually used for cutting down crops, but the Scarecrow looks like he has more sinister plans for his.

Power of Two

Two-Face is obsessed with the number two. He makes decisions on whether to act for good or evil using a double-sided coin.

Attack of the Plants

Poison Ivy lives up to her name. She can command poisonous plants and uses them to trap people and control their minds.

Grapnel Gun

Robin doesn't need wings to fly. He can scale walls and swing between skyscrapers high above the ground with his grapnel gun.

More Batarangs

Batman's Batarangs come in all shapes and sizes. Whether for climbing walls or slicing ropes, a Batarang is always useful.

Cane at the Ready

The Riddler is certainly up to no good with his question-mark-shaped accessory in hand.

BATMAN'S BATTLES

The Dark Knight has fought many battles to protect Gotham City. His enemies often lay cunning traps to try to capture him. Sometimes his trusty sidekick Robin is there to help him, but other times he has to rely on just his wits and weapons to work his way out of tricky situations. Watch out, Batman!

Ice Attack

Mr. Freeze is on the attack with his freeze ray gun. Batman will need all of his strength to break free from the ice around his ankles. Brr!

Trapped

Batman and Robin have fallen into a trap! These metal chains will be difficult to wriggle out of, but Batman looks like he has a plan.

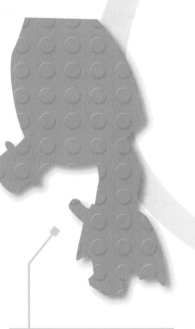

All Tied Up

The Riddler loves riddles, but he and the Penguin have a real puzzle on their hands: how are they going to escape from Batman's clutches?

Caught in a Net

The Batman has caught himself a Penguin. This net will keep the crook tightly secured and out of trouble!

The Joker's Prisoner

Batman and the Joker meet in battle time and time again. The Joker loves finding new ways to imprison his toughest foe.

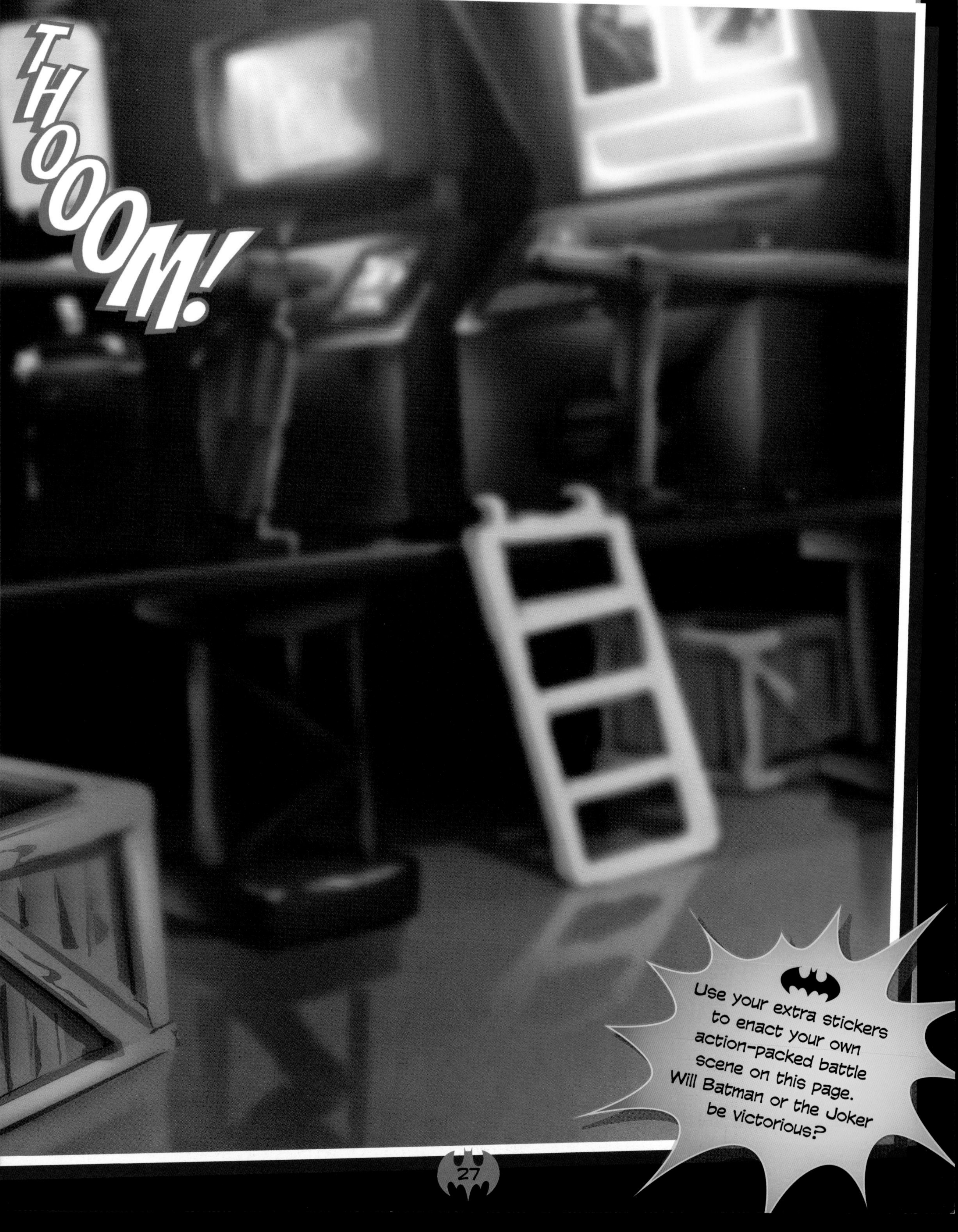
THOOOM!
Use your extra stickers to enact your own action-packed battle scene on this page. Will Batman or the Joker be victorious?

ROTTEN ROBBERS

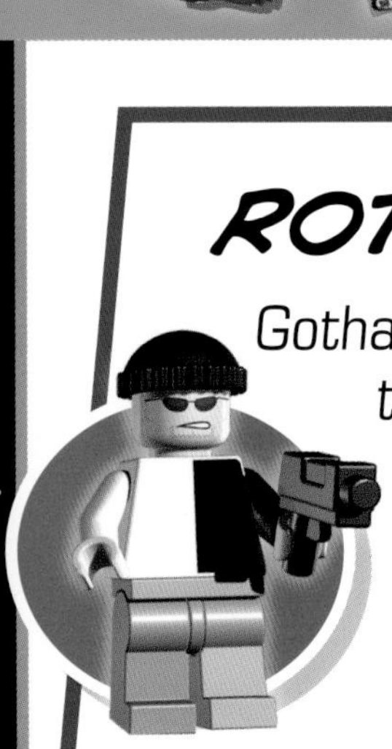

Gotham City is full of rogues who only care for themselves. They will steal anything and everything if they can, so residents had better lock up their valuables. Batman has his work cut out for him trying to catch this bunch of rotten robbers!

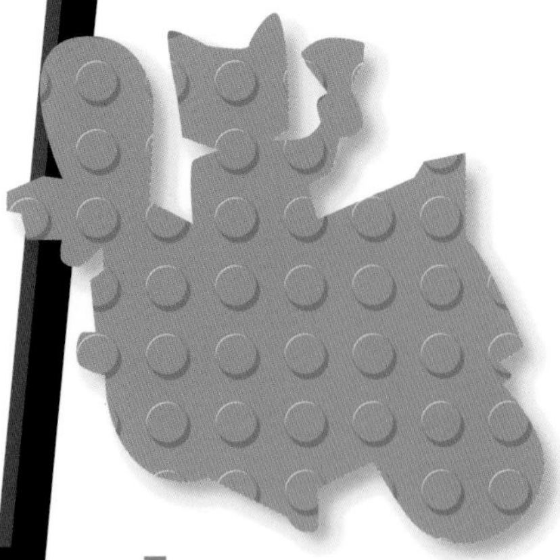

Double Trouble

With his love of pairs, Two-Face has two evil henchmen to assist him. They wear identical two-tone outfits and matching grimaces.

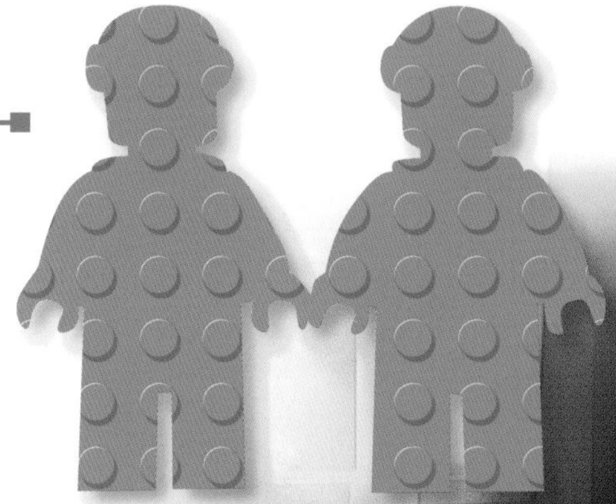

Cat-burglar

Catwoman can't resist stealing a shiny diamond. She uses her customized Catcycle to make a quick getaway.

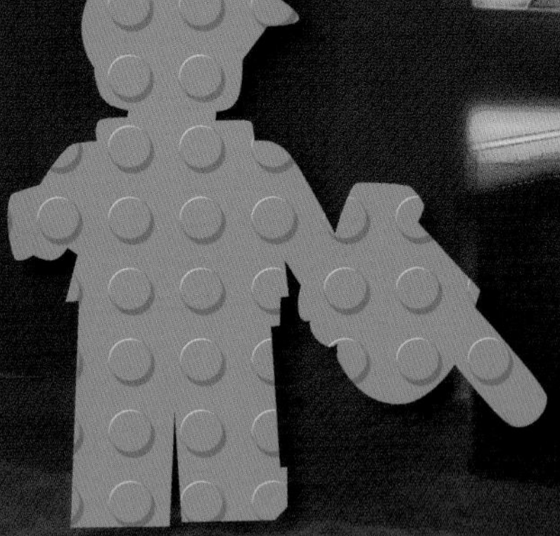

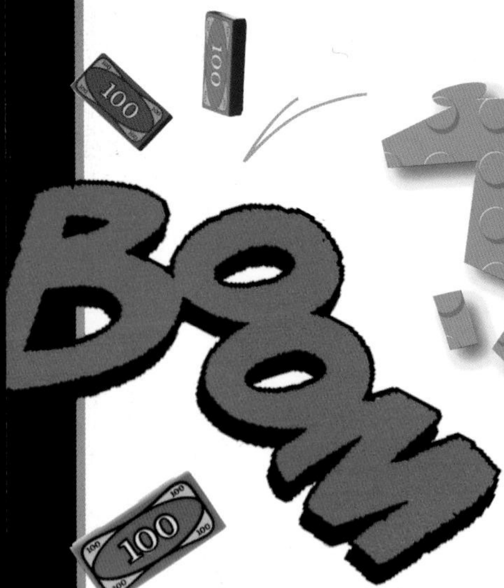
BOOM
100
100
100

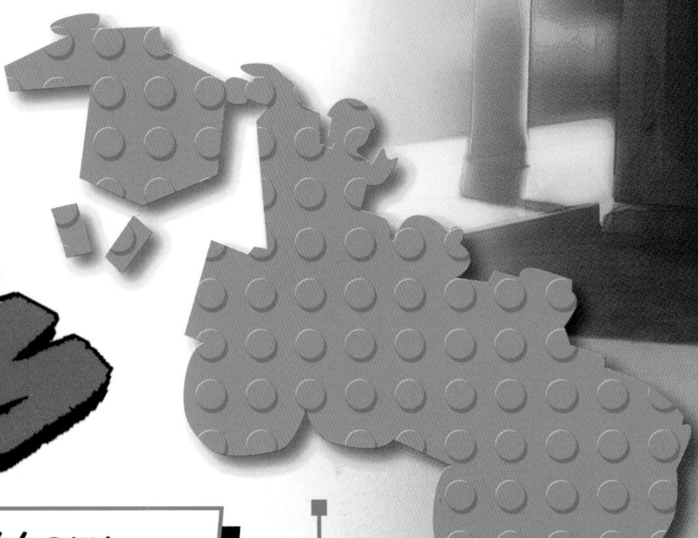

At Gunpoint

Two-Face has been involved in many hold-ups. His suit might have changed over the years but his mean attitude hasn't.

Bank Robbery

Raise the alarm! Two-Face and his henchmen have broken into the bank and are zooming off with the safe. Will Batman stop them in time?

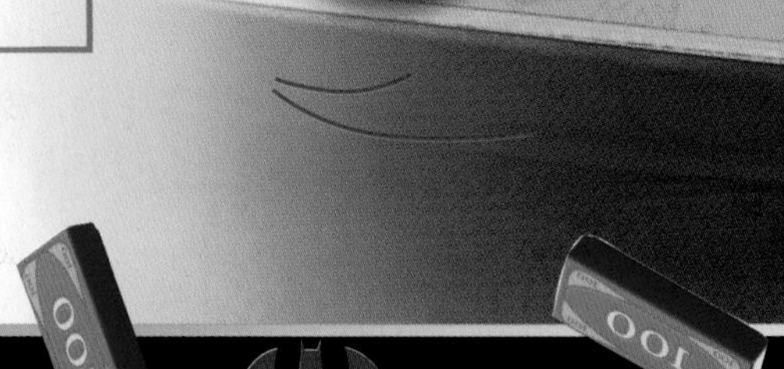
100
100

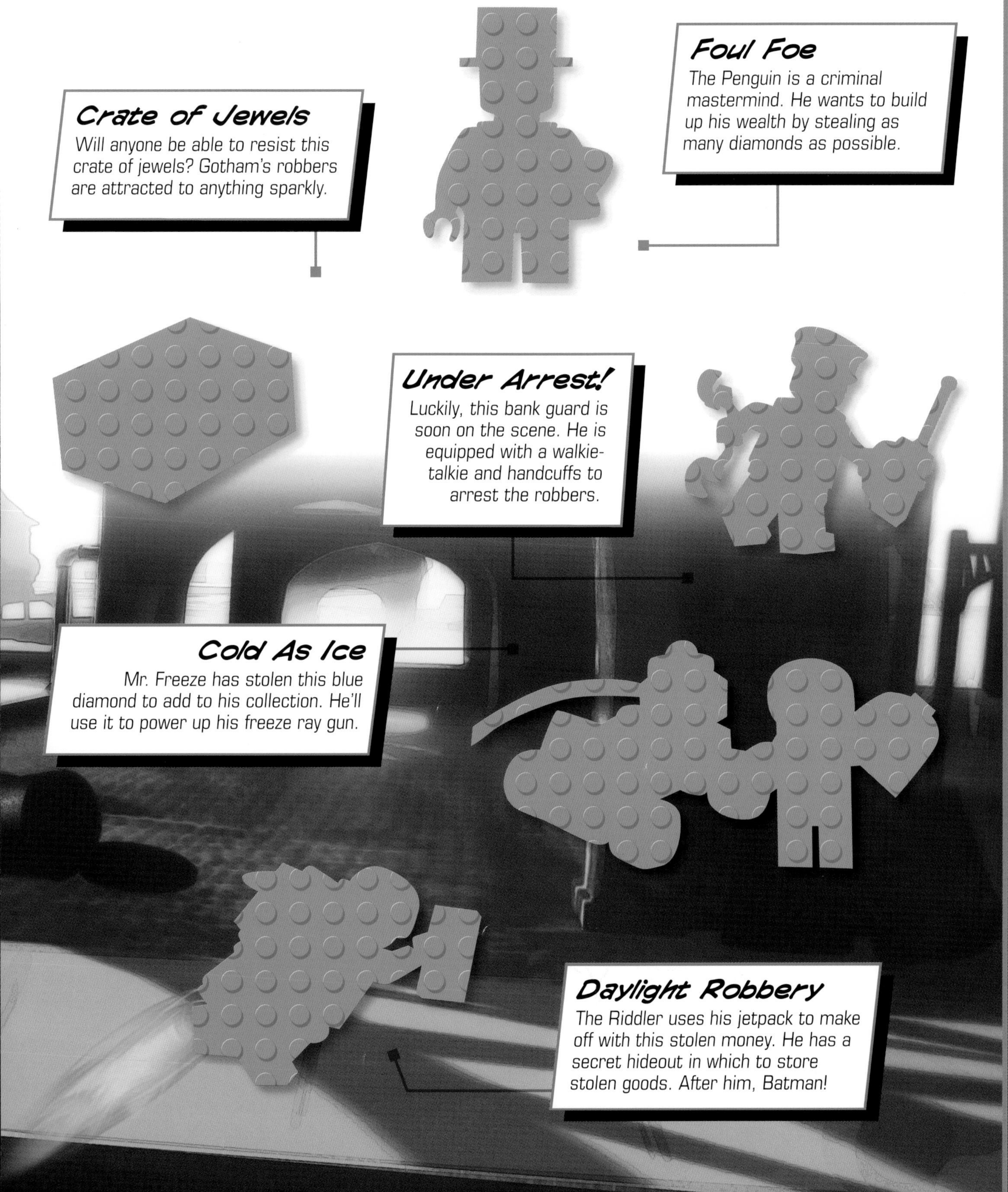

Crate of Jewels

Will anyone be able to resist this crate of jewels? Gotham's robbers are attracted to anything sparkly.

Foul Foe

The Penguin is a criminal mastermind. He wants to build up his wealth by stealing as many diamonds as possible.

Under Arrest!

Luckily, this bank guard is soon on the scene. He is equipped with a walkie-talkie and handcuffs to arrest the robbers.

Cold As Ice

Mr. Freeze has stolen this blue diamond to add to his collection. He'll use it to power up his freeze ray gun.

Daylight Robbery

The Riddler uses his jetpack to make off with this stolen money. He has a secret hideout in which to store stolen goods. After him, Batman!

AT THE FUNHOUSE

On the outskirts of Gotham City lies the Joker's lair: a run-down theme park called the Funhouse. It is the ideal secret location for the Joker to plot his mad schemes. With the help of Harley Quinn and the Riddler, he has captured Robin. Will Batman rescue his sidekick in time?

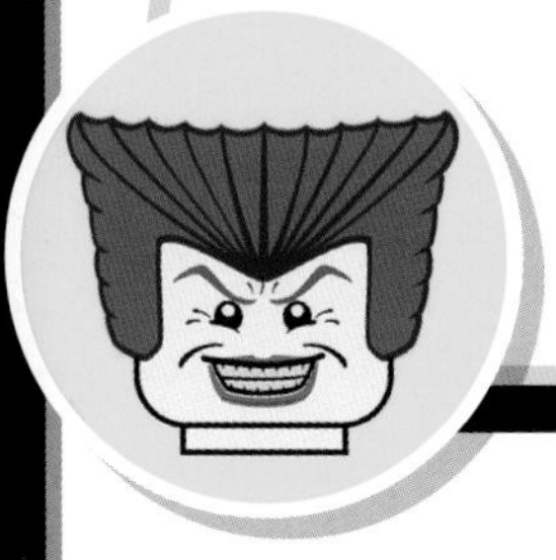

Puzzling

The Funhouse is the perfect place for the Riddler and his love of tricks. There are trap doors, giant hammers, and moving floors to avoid.

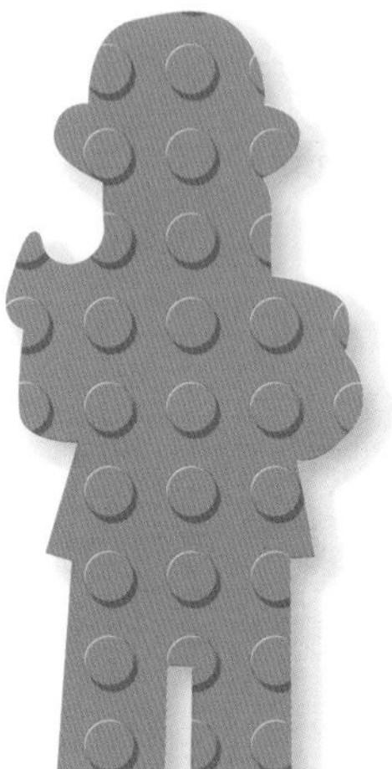

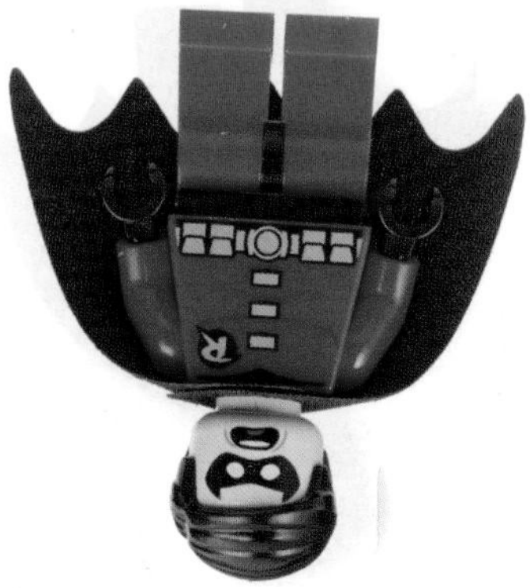

Captured Robin

Behind Robin's mask is a face of pure terror. Somehow he has found himself held upside down as the Joker's prisoner.

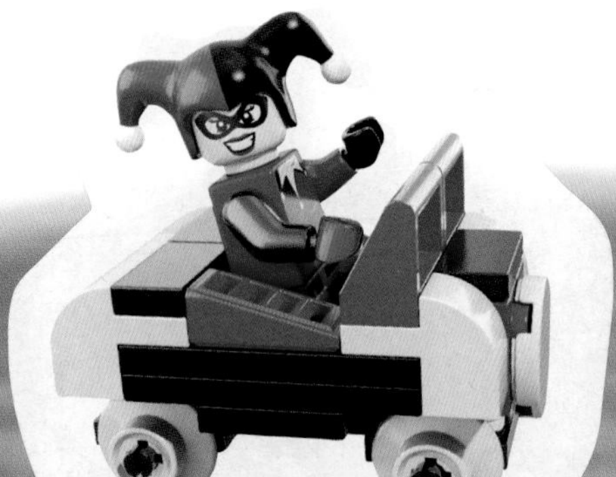

Theme Park Ride

Hold on tight! Harley Quinn rides a loose rollercoaster car and is ready to zoom down the Funhouse's tracks.

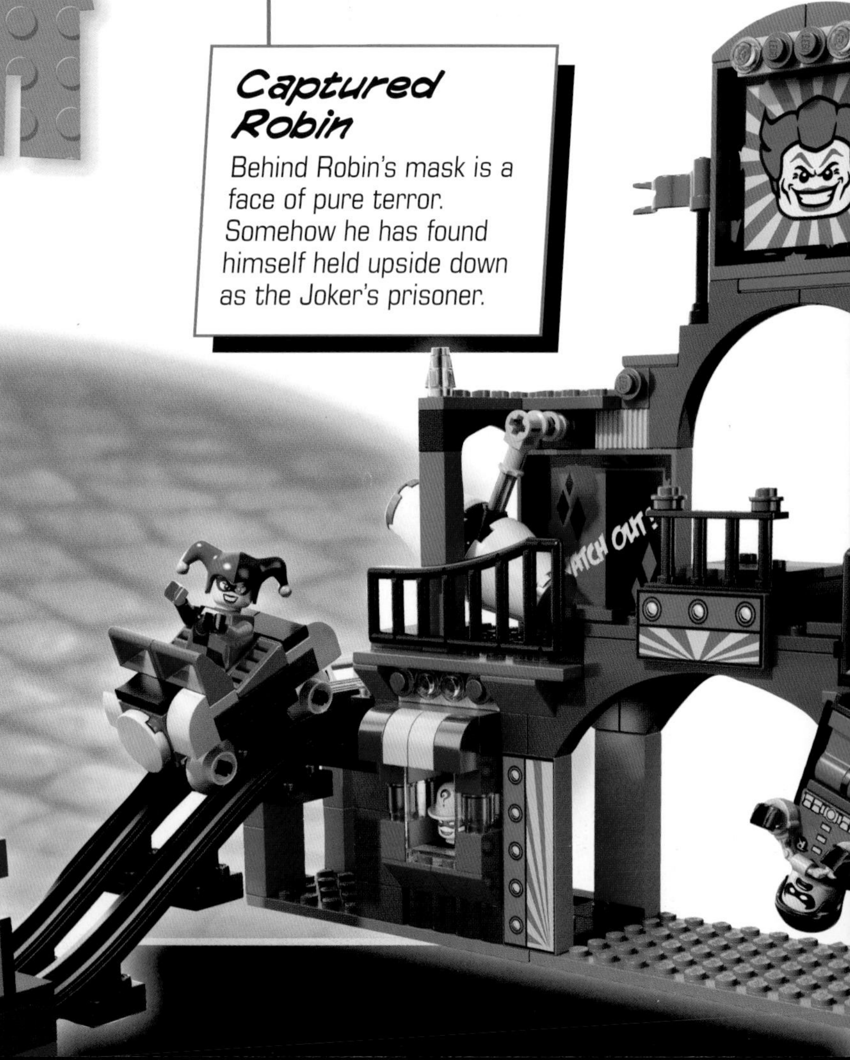

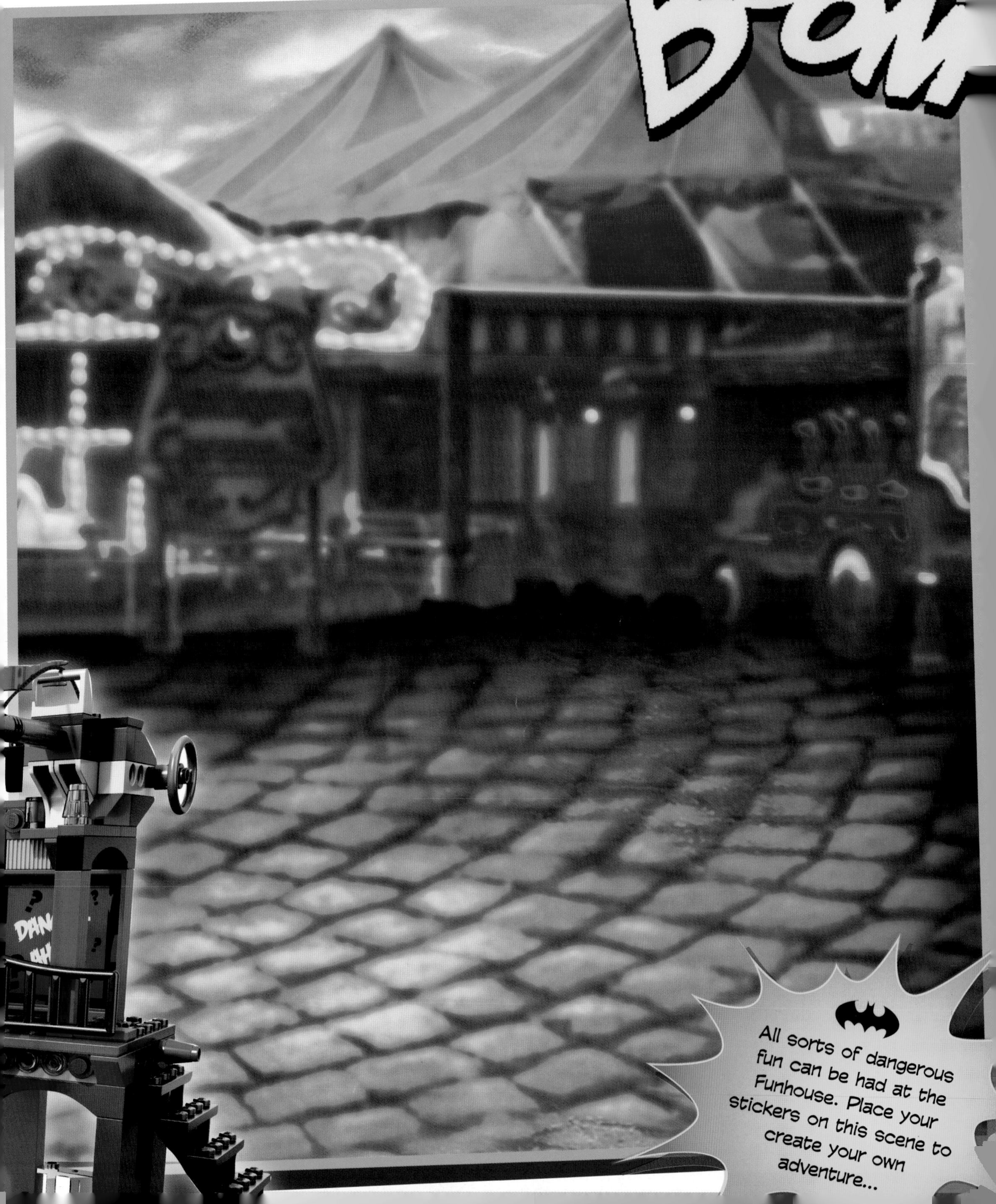

All sorts of dangerous fun can be had at the Funhouse. Place your stickers on this scene to create your own adventure...

SUPER HEROES & VILLAINS

Batman has allies all around the world, not just in Gotham City. These super heroes come to his aid whenever he needs them, and the Caped Crusader is always happy to return the favor. Unfortunately, these friends sometimes bring with them a few extra enemies...

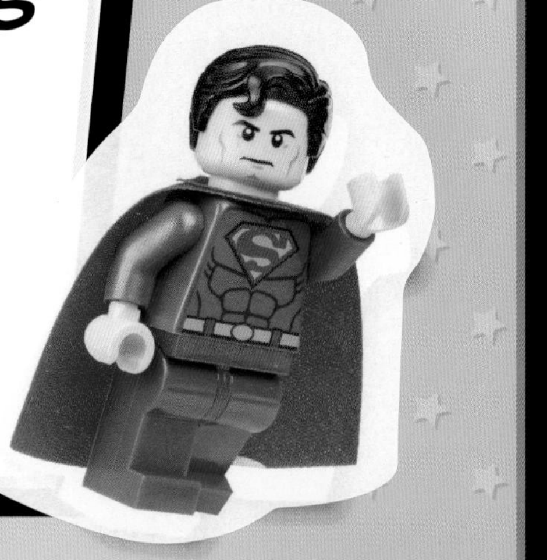

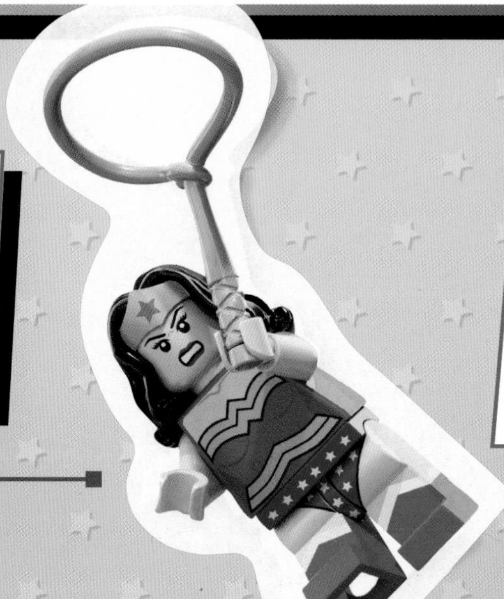

Wonder Woman

Wonder Woman is not to be messed with! The fierce Amazon Princess will charge to the rescue with her golden Lasso of Truth.

Superman

Superman and Batman have worked together many times to tackle troublesome foes. If called, the Man of Steel will fly straight to Batman's aid.

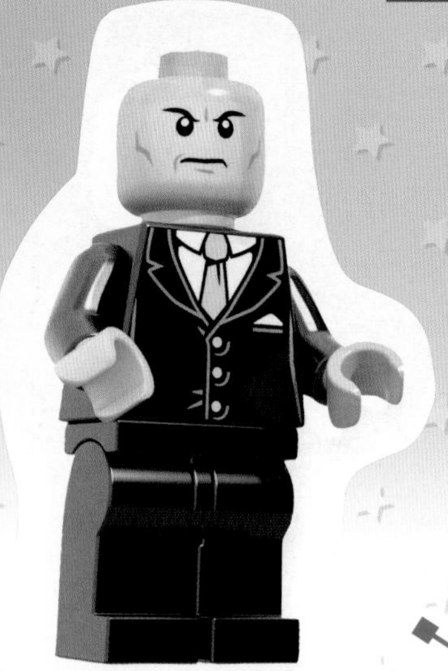

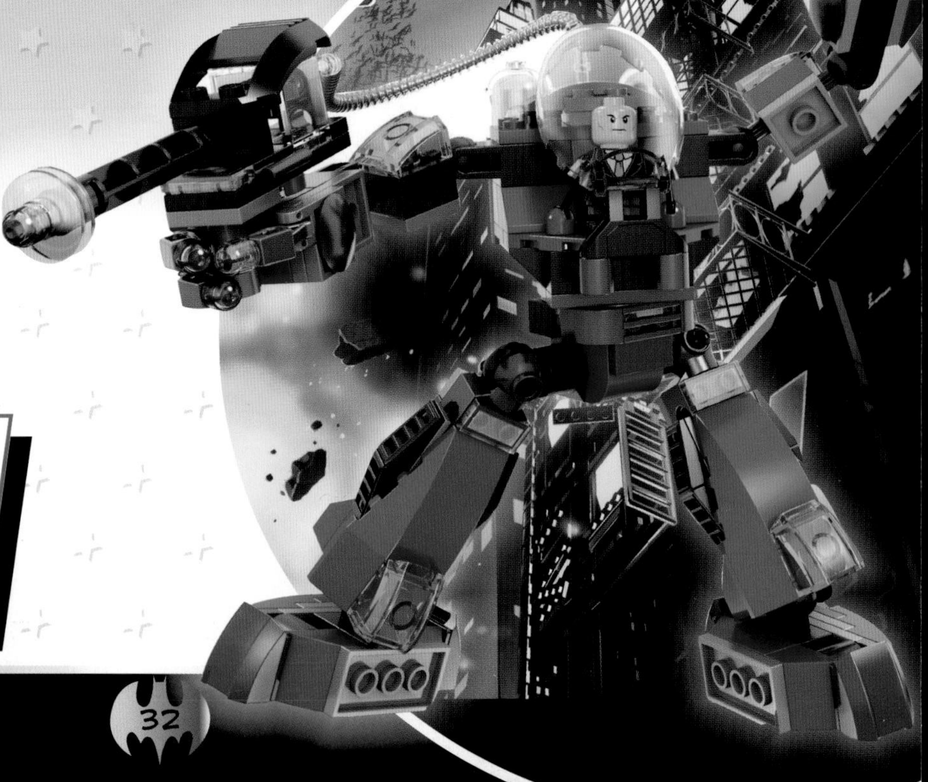

Lex Luthor

Lex Luthor is Superman's archenemy. Sometimes he likes to cause trouble in Gotham too—using his genius mind and hi-tech robotic weapons.

STICKERS

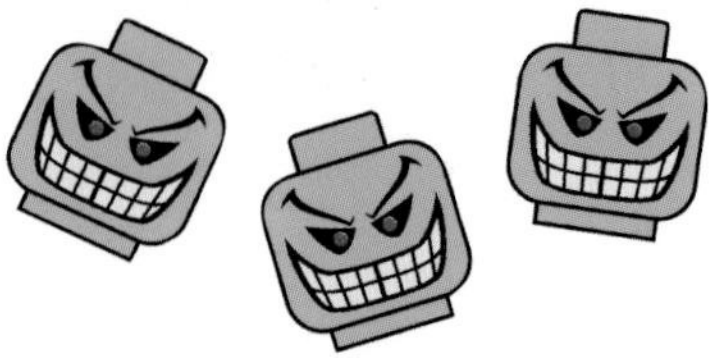

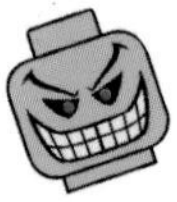

Poison Ivy

Two-Face

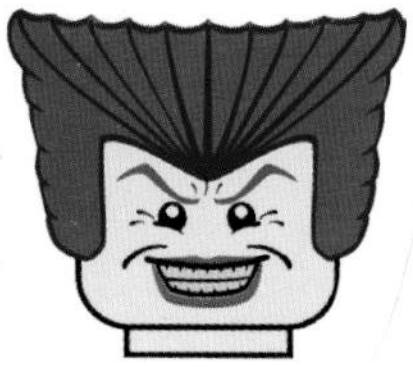

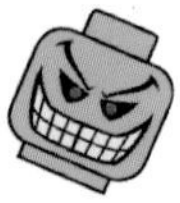

The Scarecrow

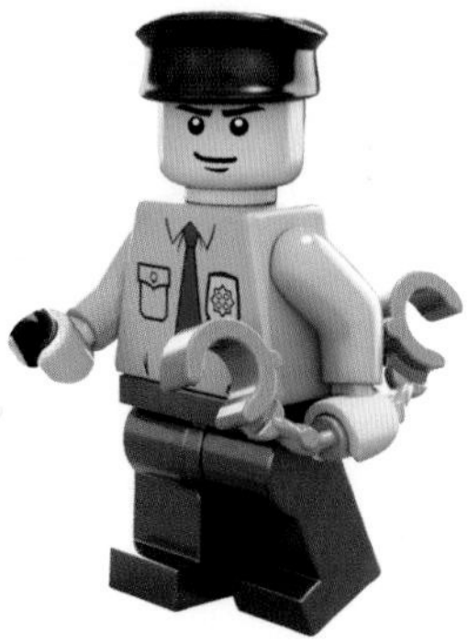

Catwoman

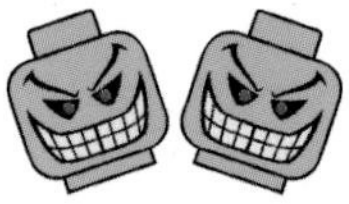

Harley Quinn

Bane

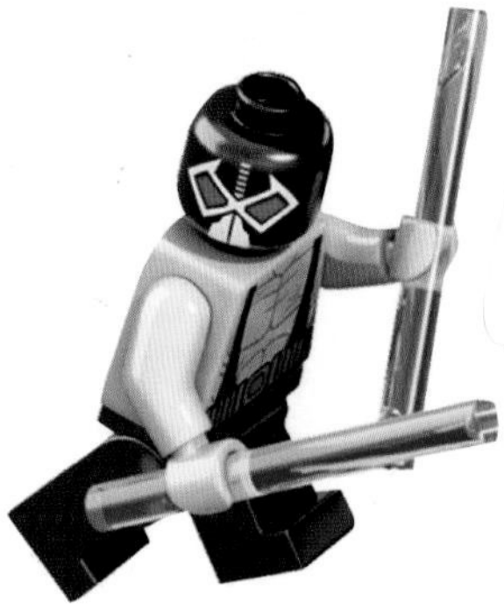

The Riddler

The Penguin

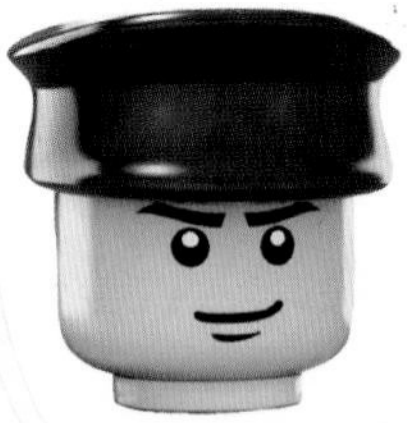

STICKERS

Killer Croc

The Joker

Mr. Freeze

Ivy's Tower

Keeping Watch

Bank Guard

Patients' Ward

Arkham Asylum

STICKERS

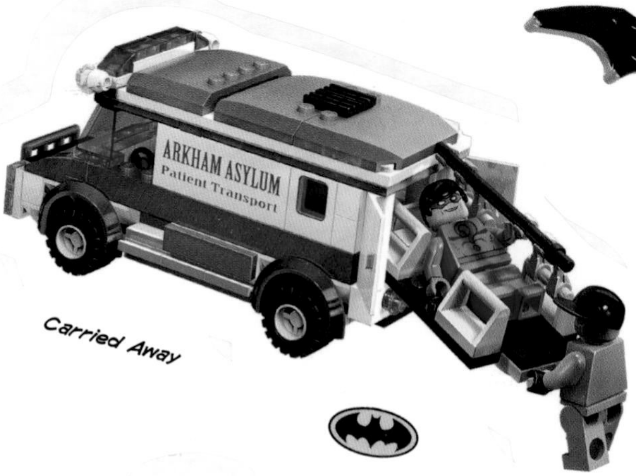
ARKHAM ASYLUM
Patient Transport

Carried Away

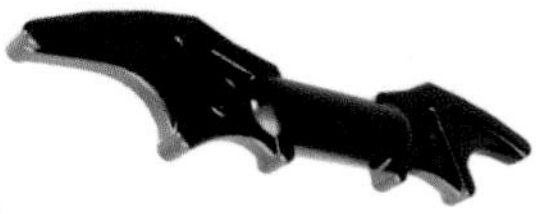

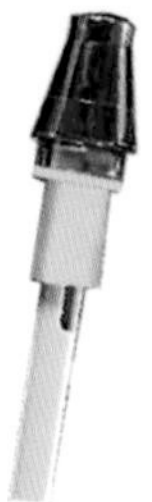

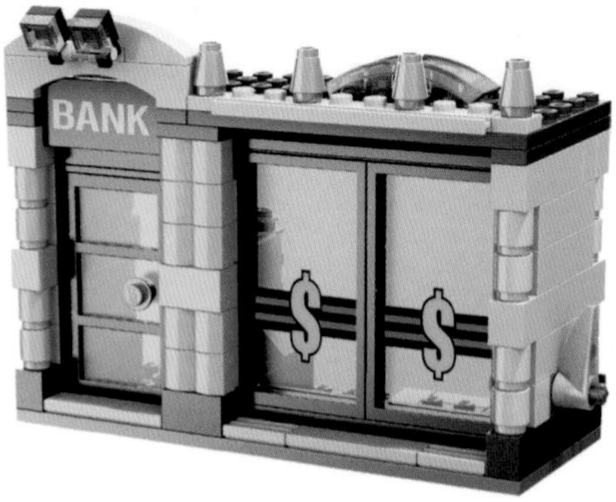
BANK

At the Bank

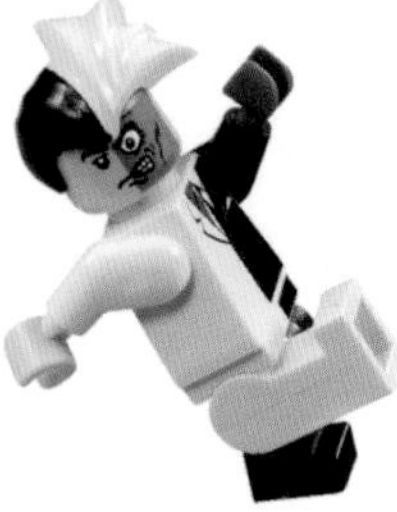

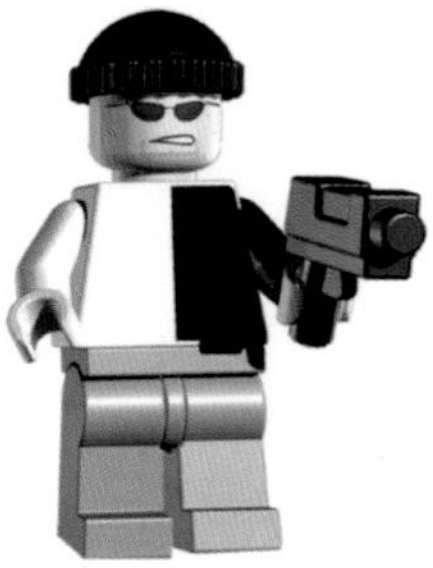

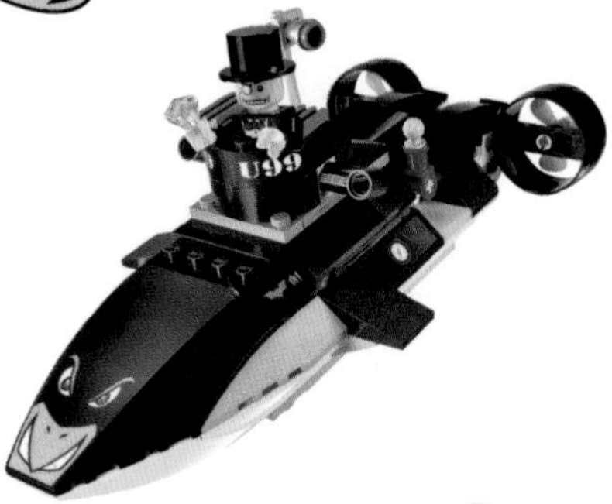

Asylum Guards

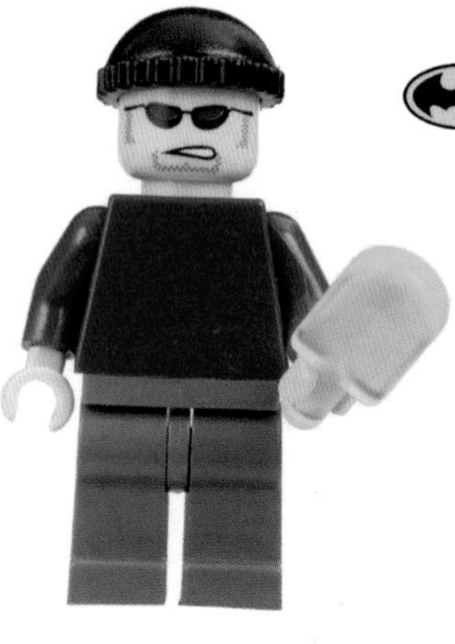

Venomous

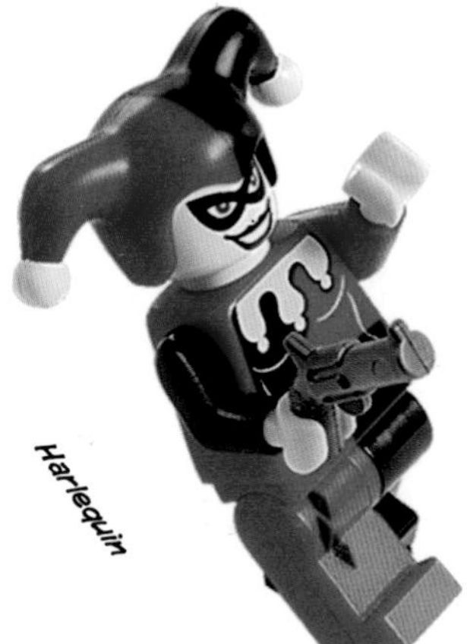

Harlequin

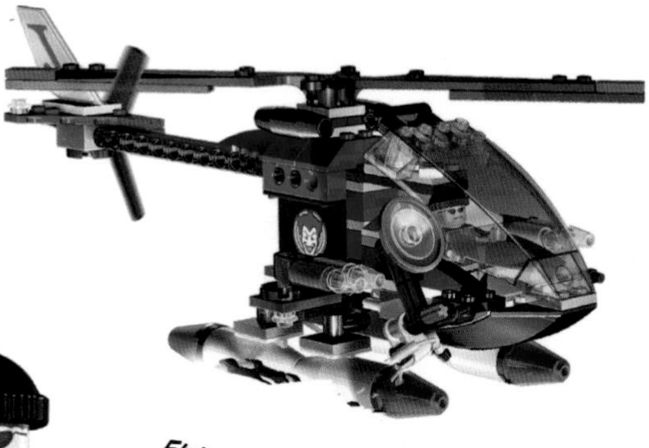

Flying High

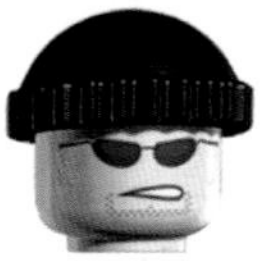

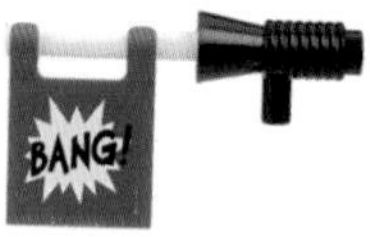
BANG!

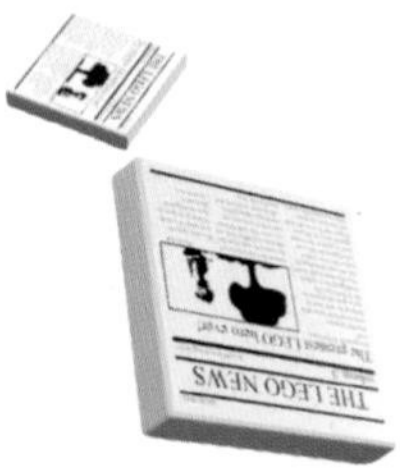

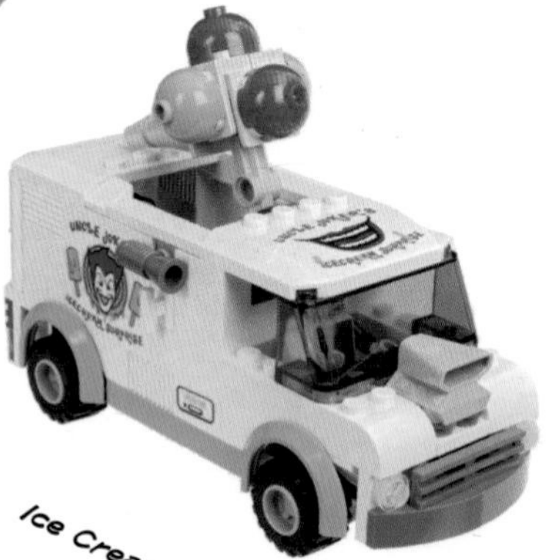

Ice Cream Truck

Joke Bomb

STICKERS

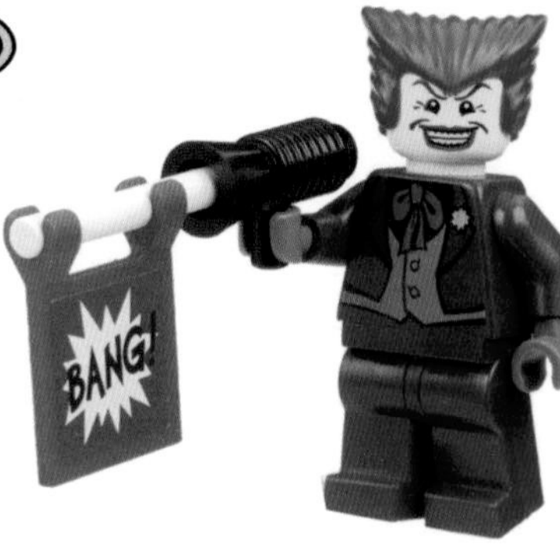
BANG!

"Bang!"

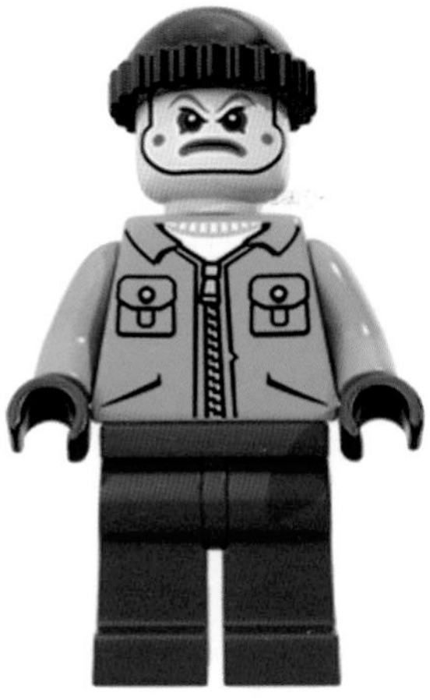

Clowning Around

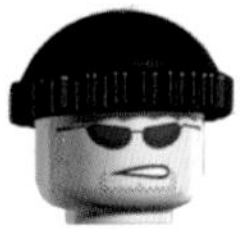

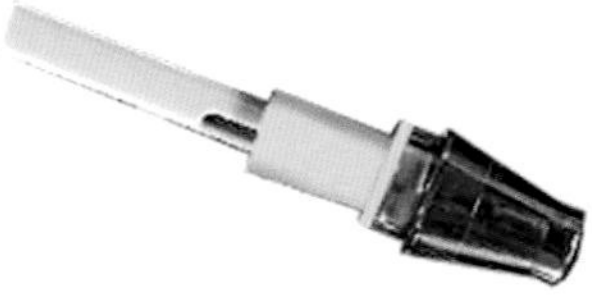

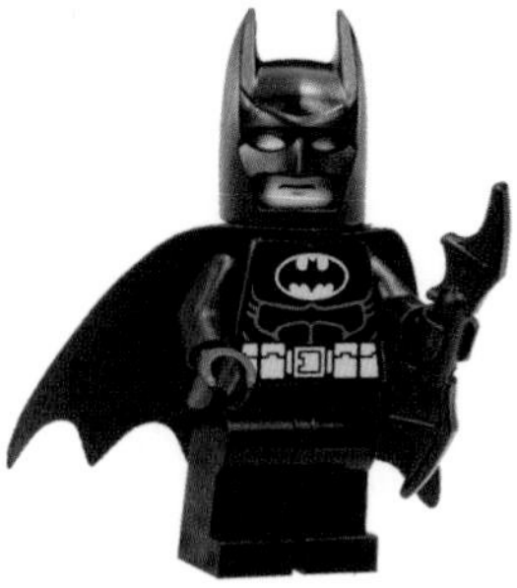

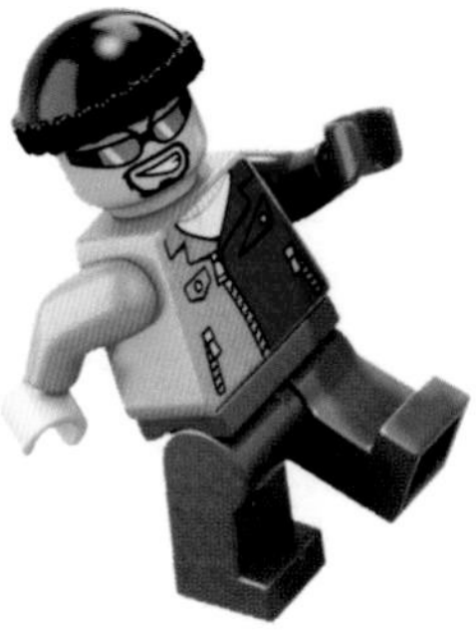

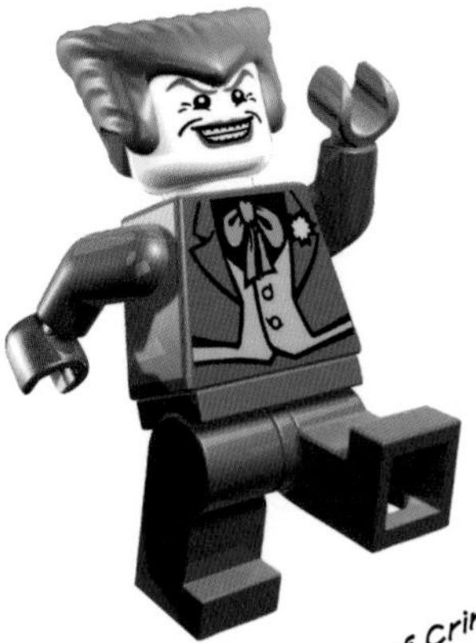

Clown Prince of Crime

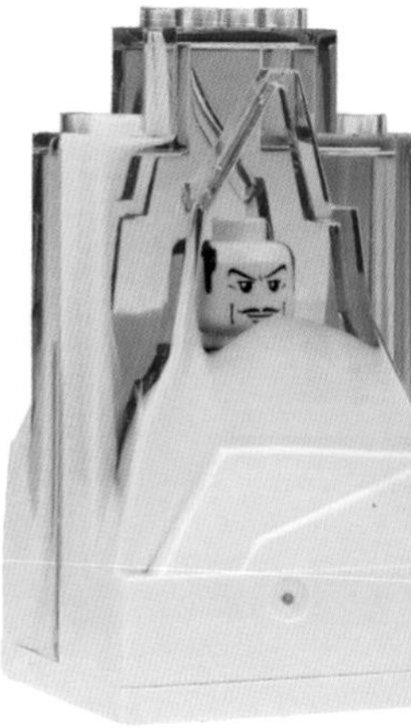

Frozen in Ice

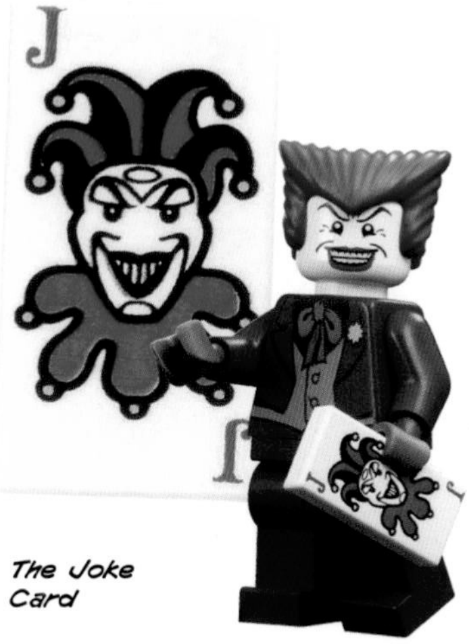

The Joke Card

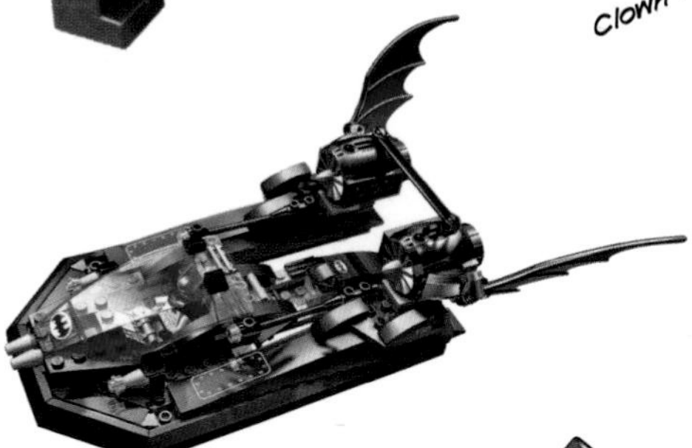

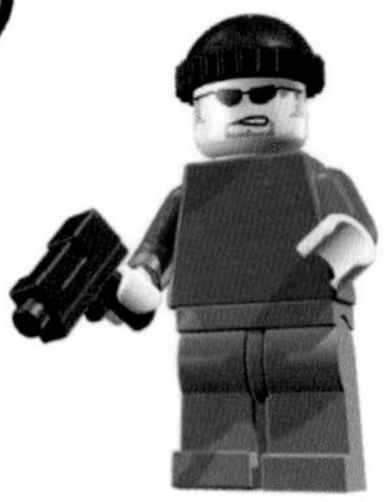

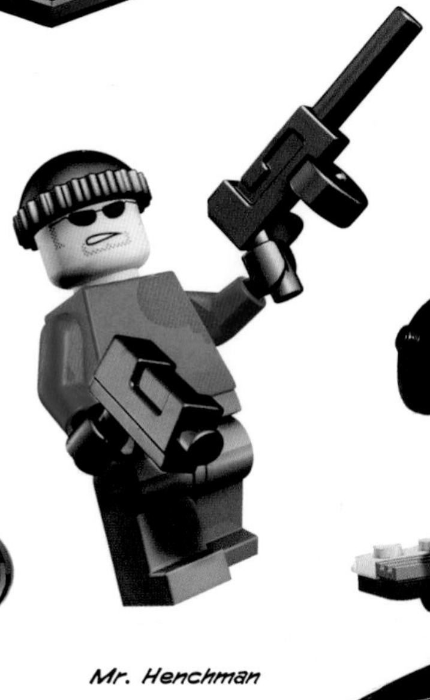

Mr. Henchman

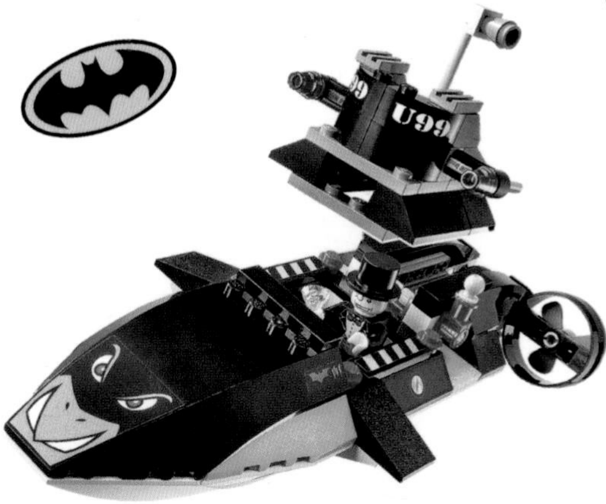
U99

Submarine

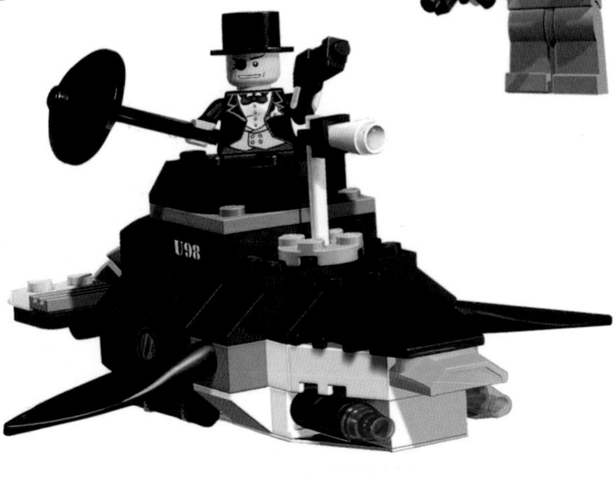
U98

Missile-firing Sub

STICKERS

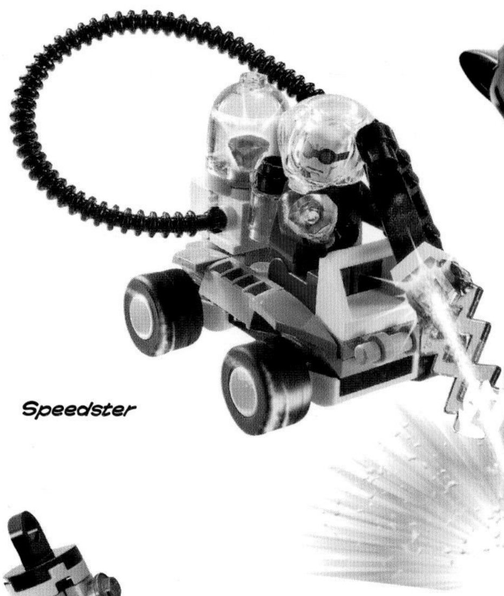

Speedster

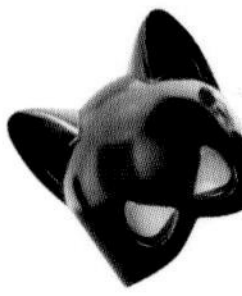

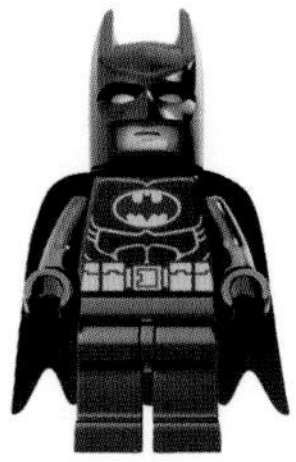

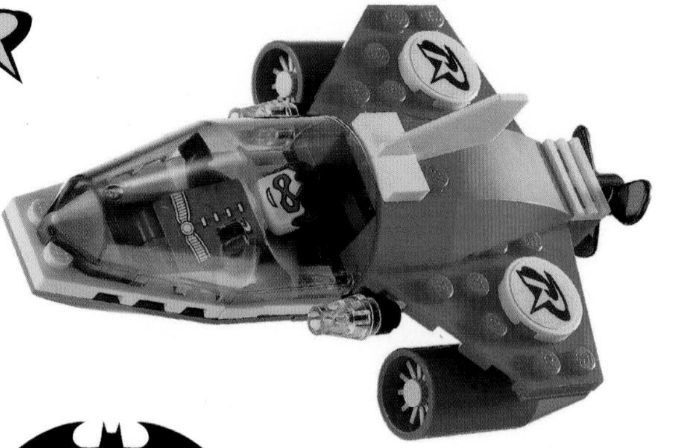

Robin's Submarine

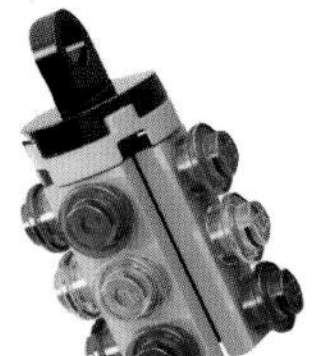

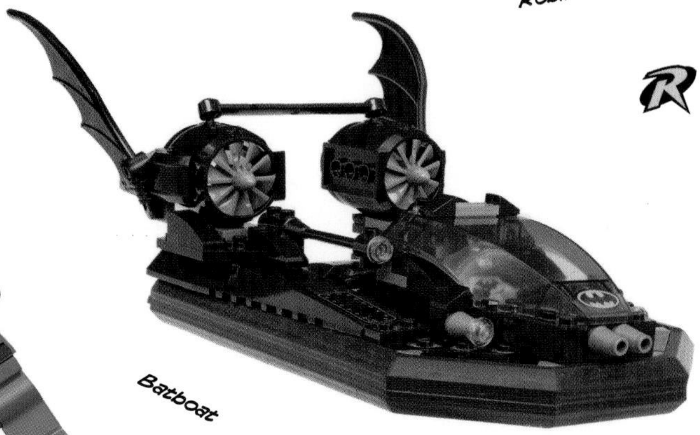

Batboat

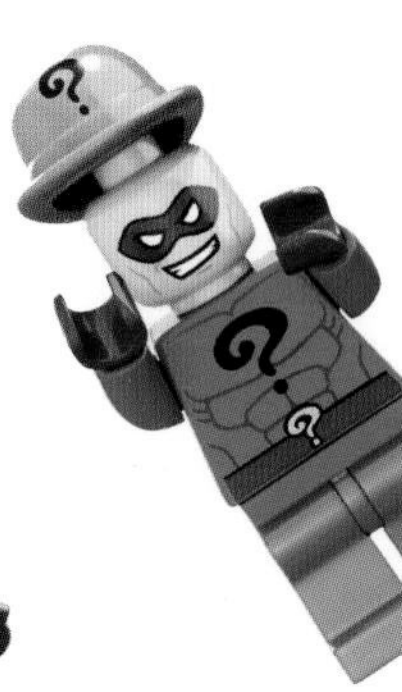

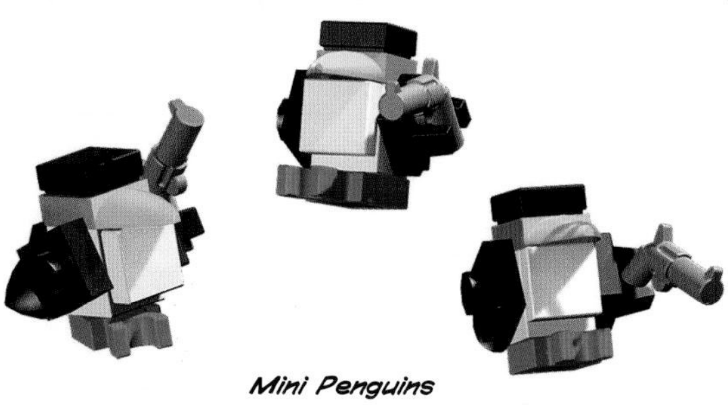

Mini Penguins

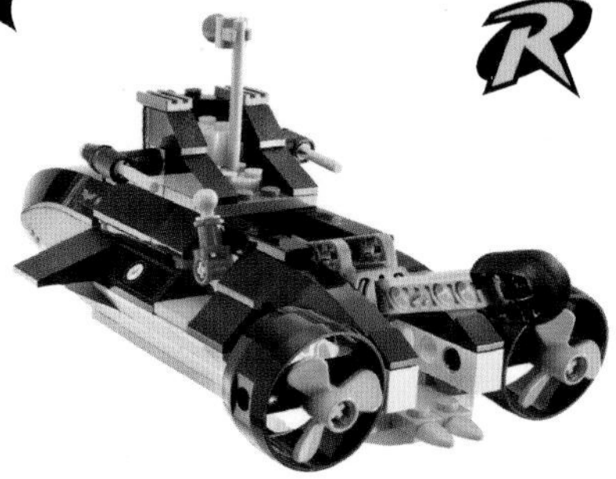

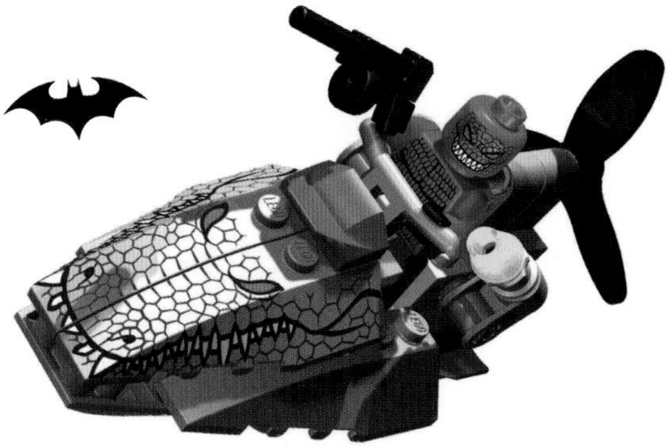

Swamp Killer

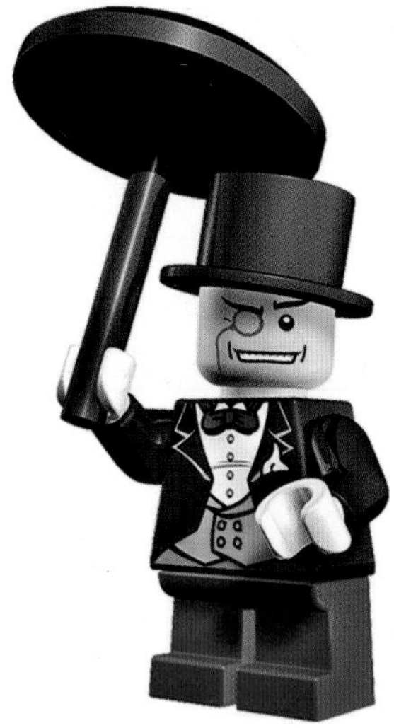

Under his Umbrella

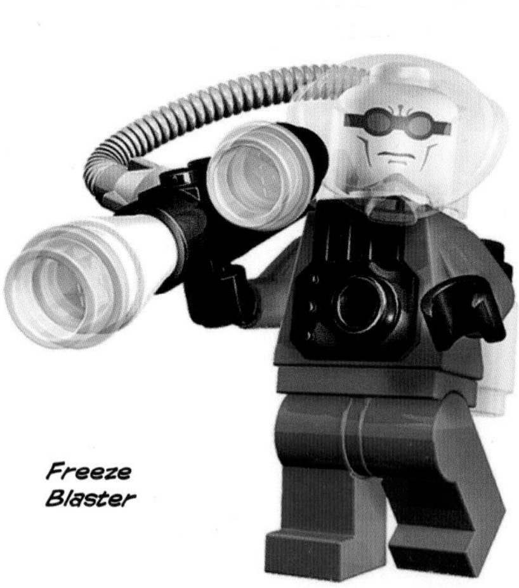

Freeze Blaster

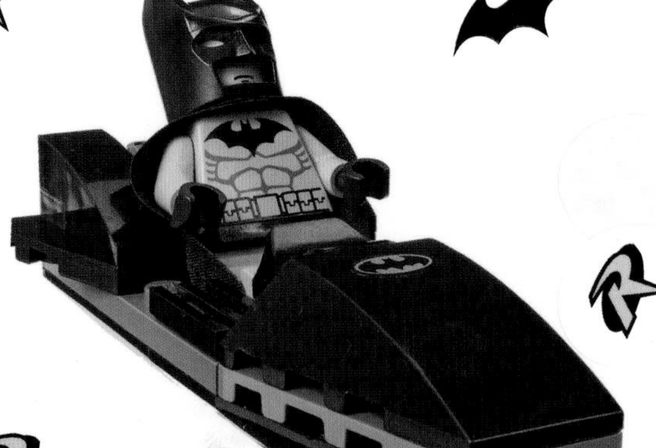

Batman's Jet Ski

STICKERS

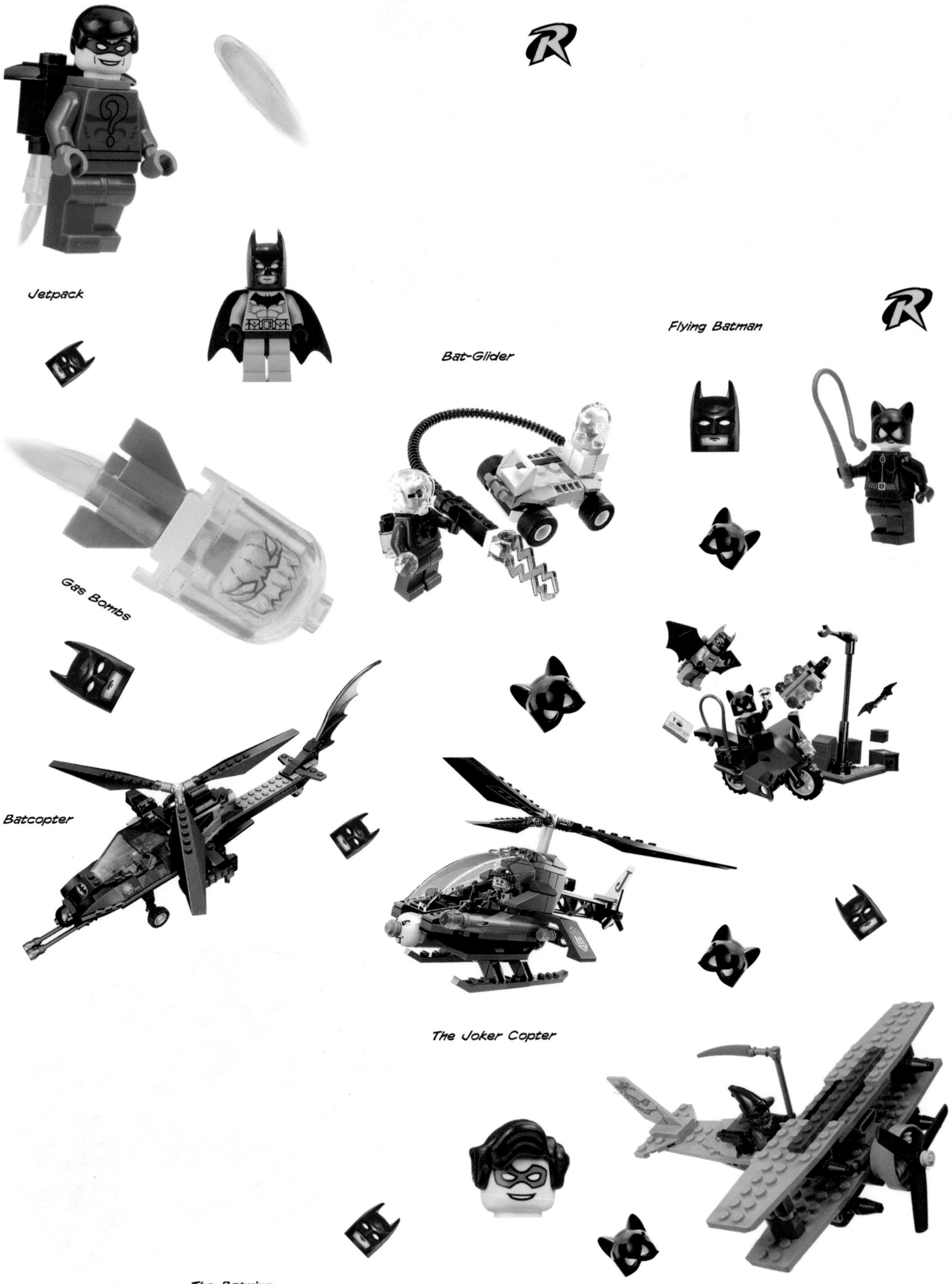

Jetpack
Flying Batman
Bat-Glider
Gas Bombs
Batcopter
The Joker Copter
The Batwing
Biplane

STICKERS

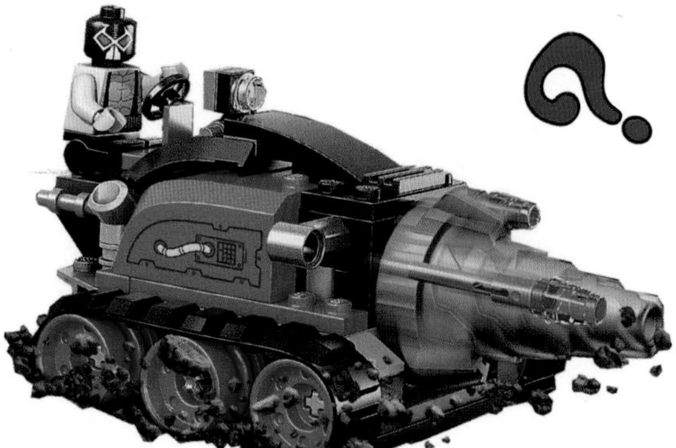
Spinning Drill Tank

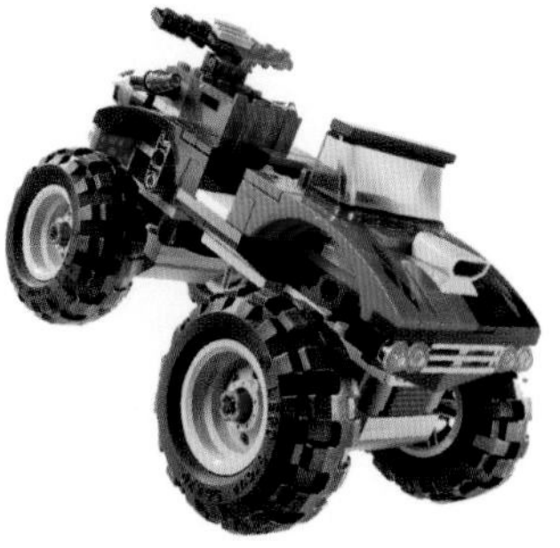

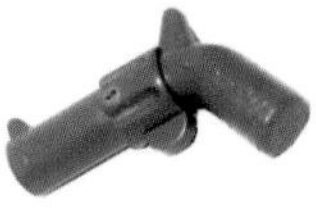

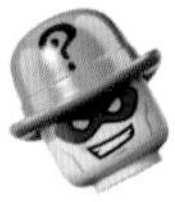

Captured Robin

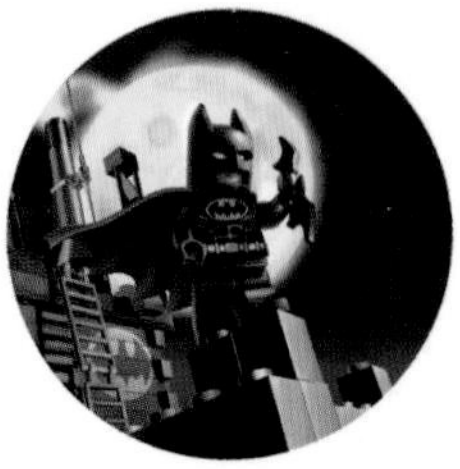

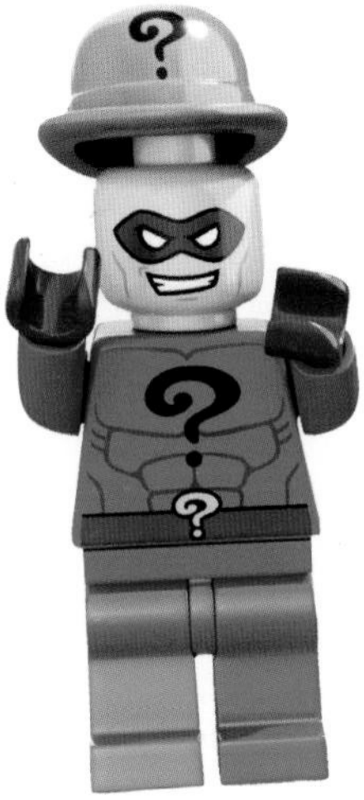

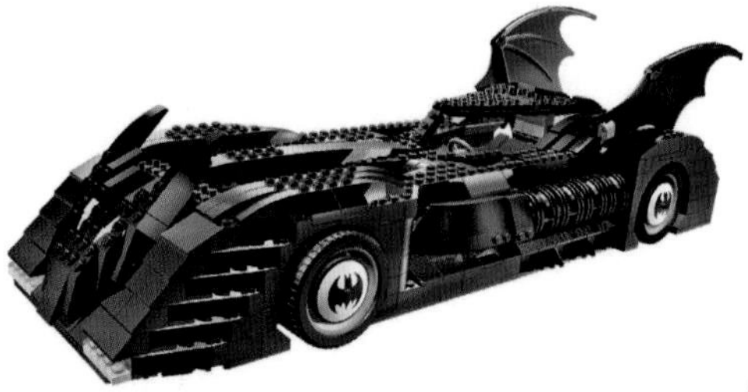

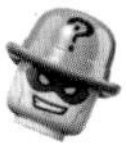

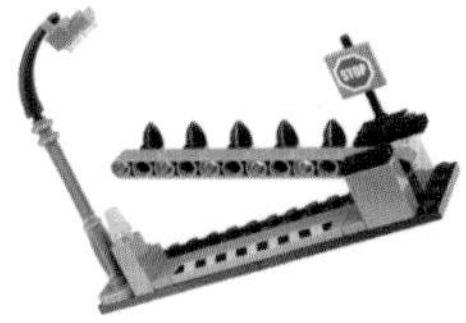

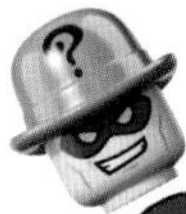

Puzzling

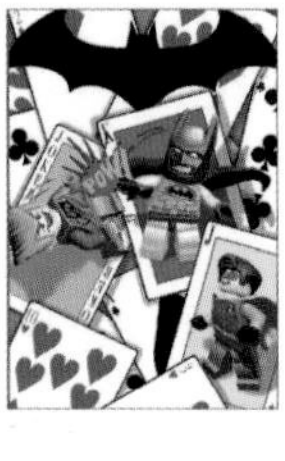

Theme Park Ride

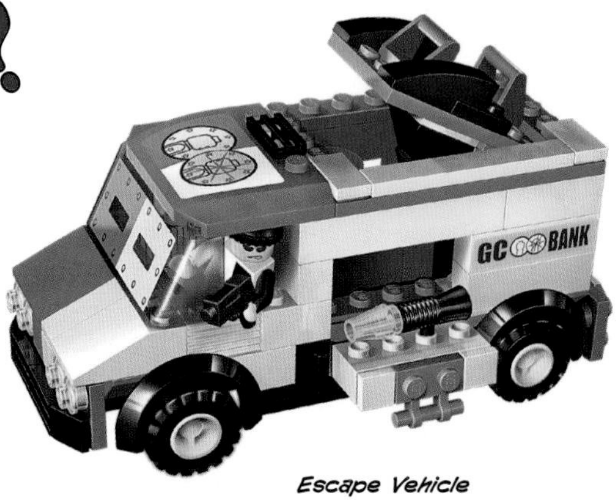
GC BANK
Escape Vehicle

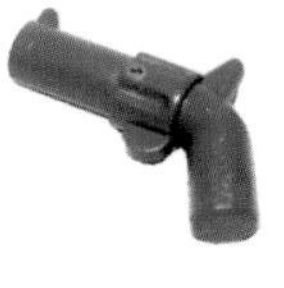

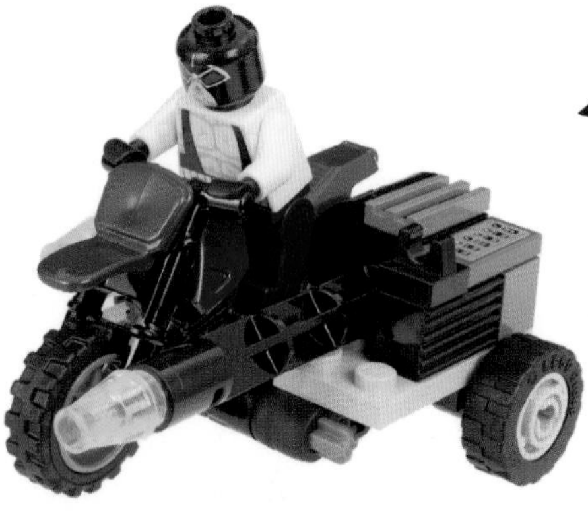
Bane's Bike

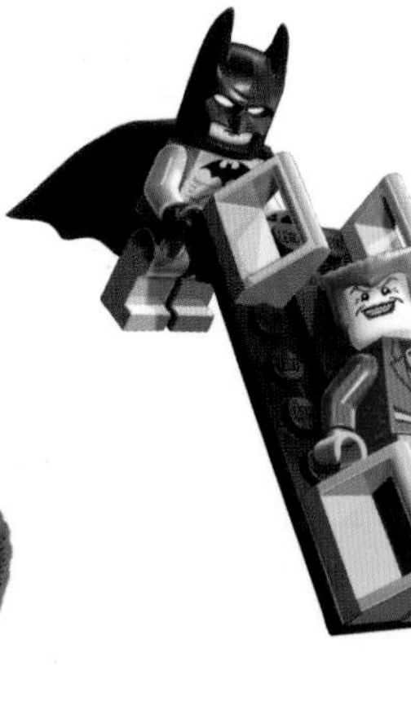

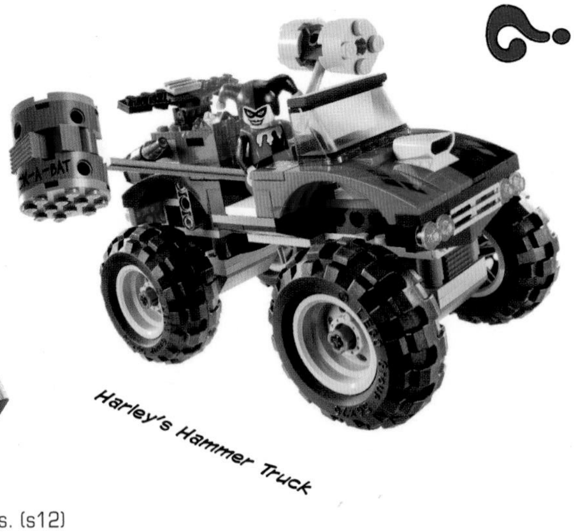
Harley's Hammer Truck

STICKERS

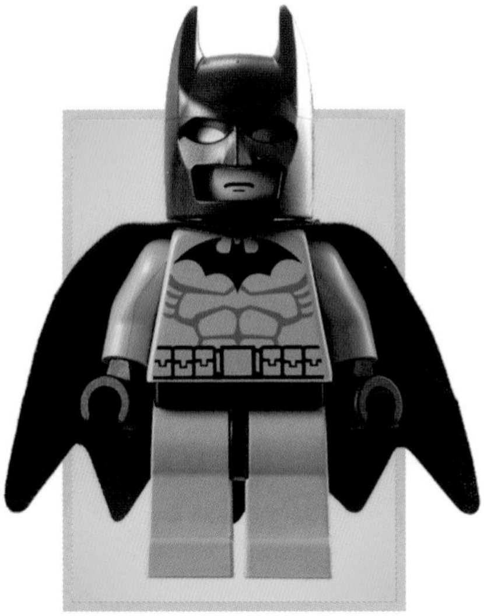

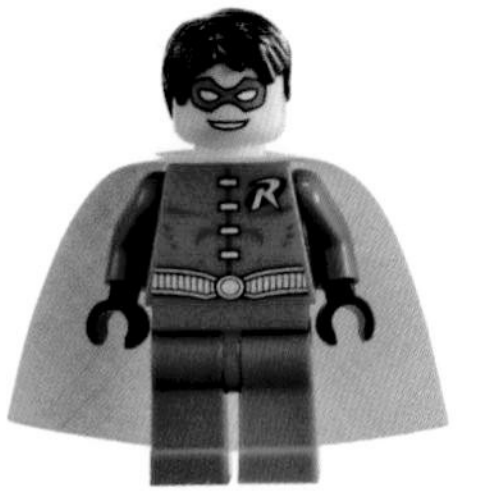

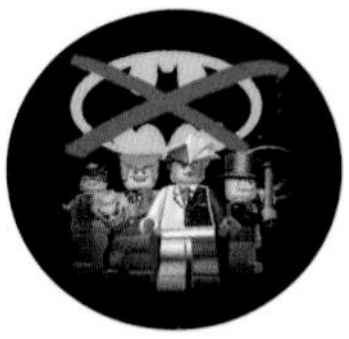

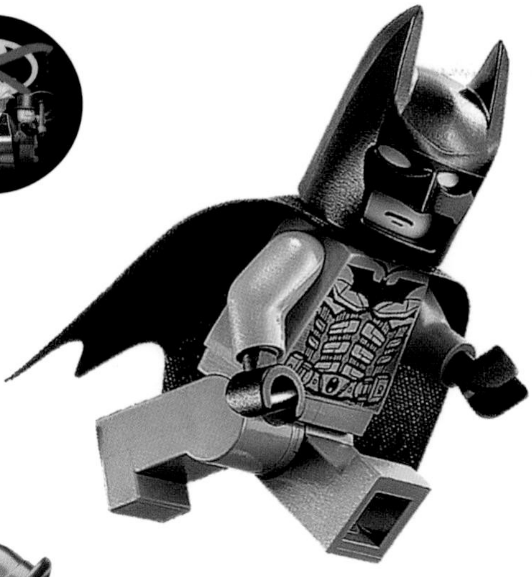

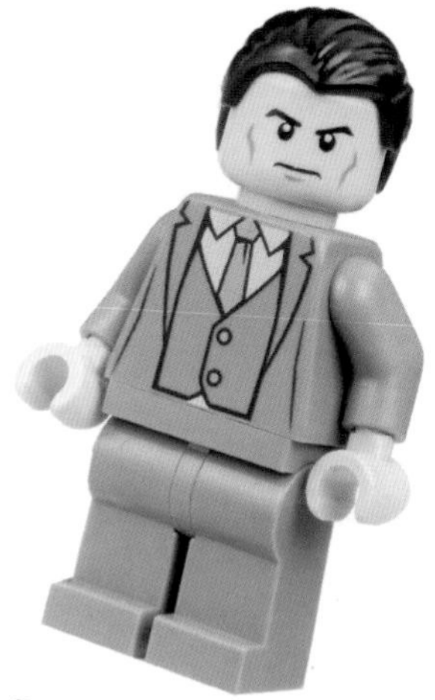

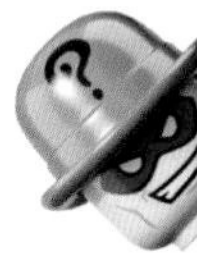

Detective

Ready for Battle

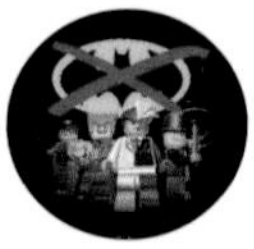

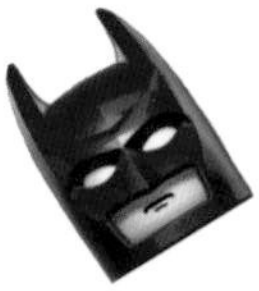

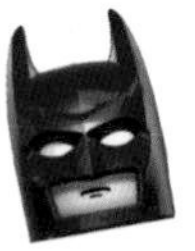

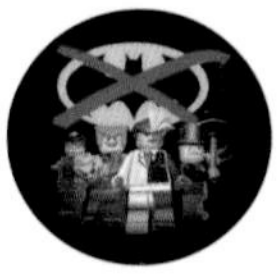

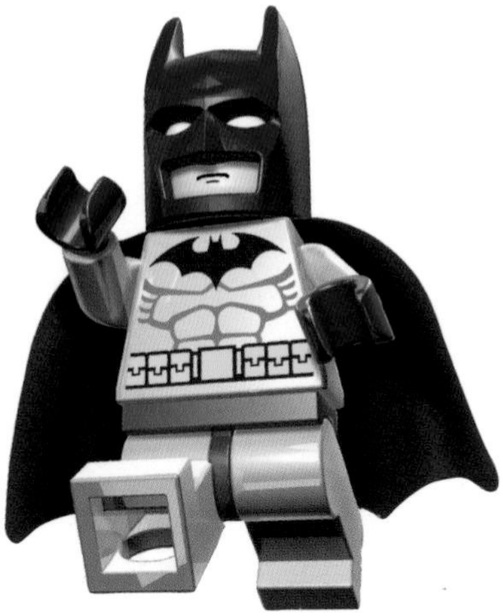

Bruce Wayne

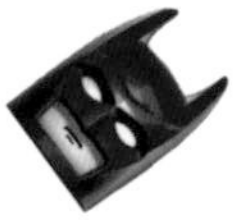

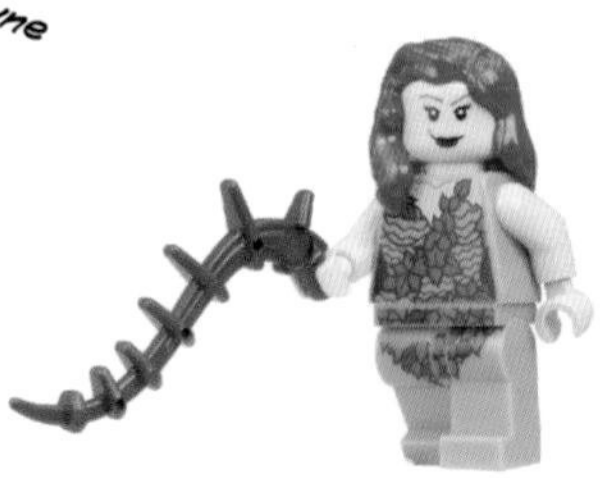

The Man in Black

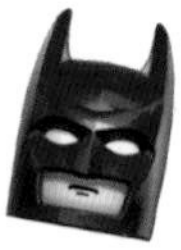

Feeling Blue

Batarangs

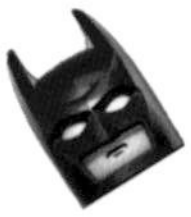

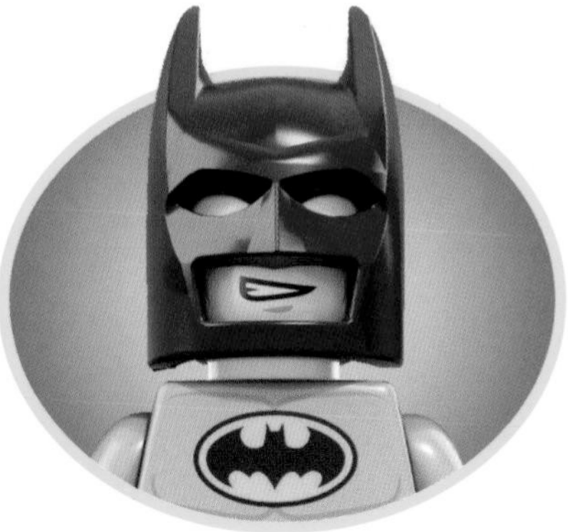

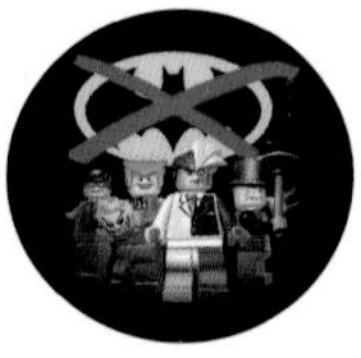

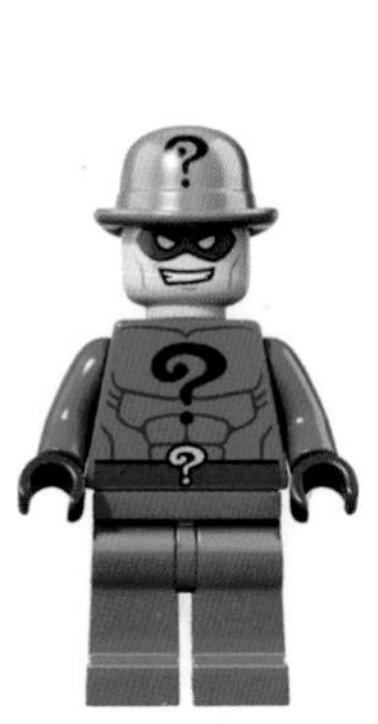

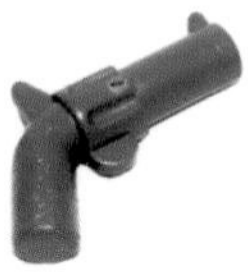

Joking Around

Bat-symbol

STICKERS

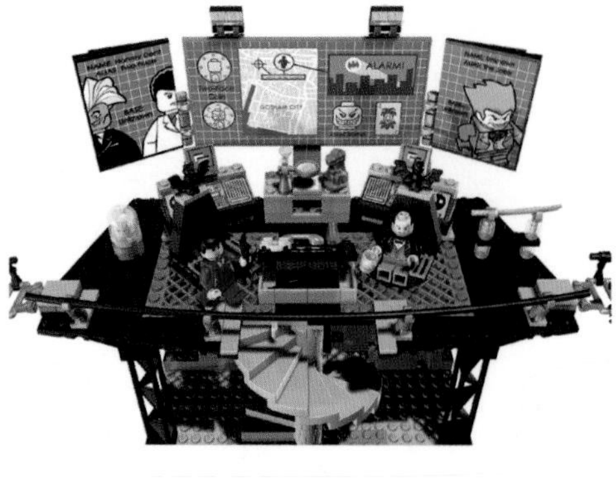

Batcomputer

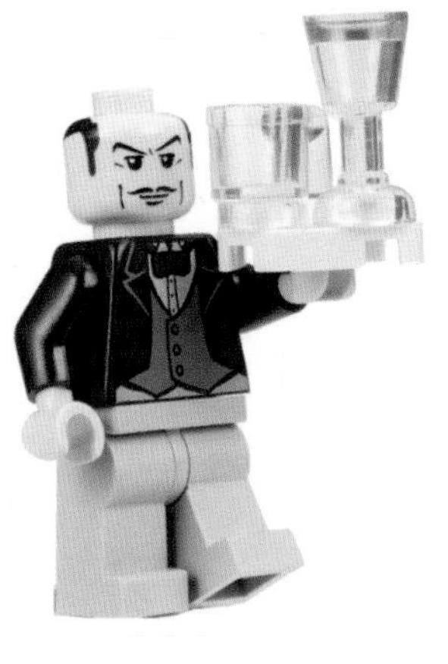

Service, Please!

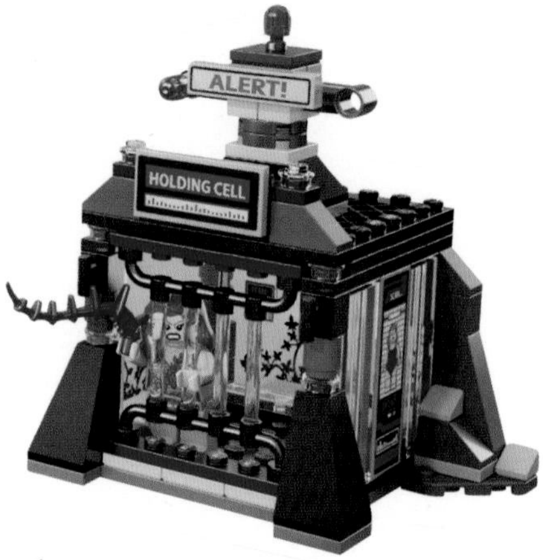
ALERT!
HOLDING CELL

Locked Up

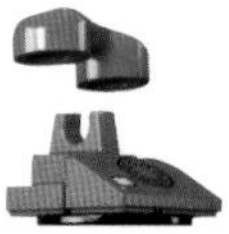

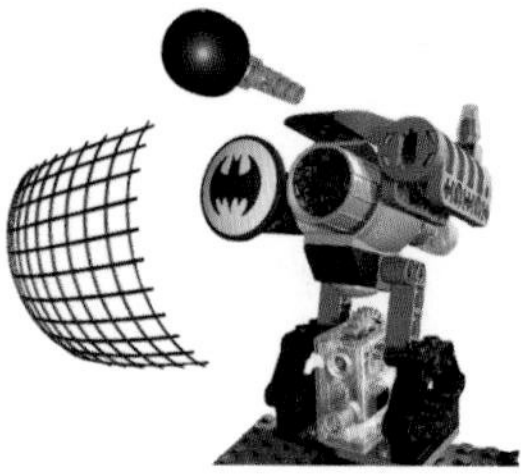

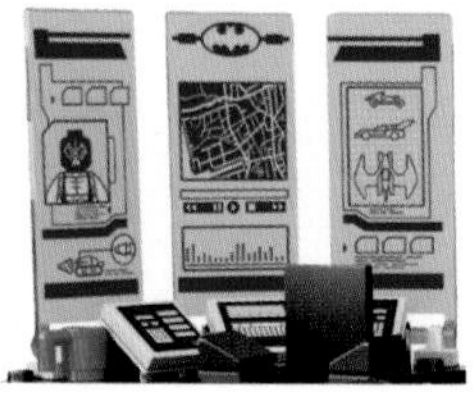

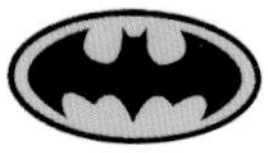

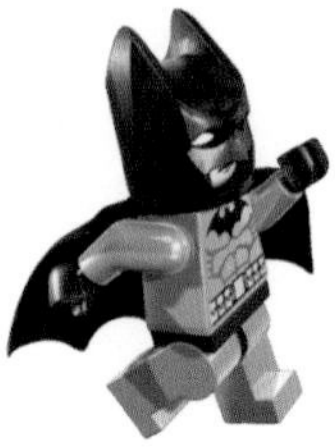

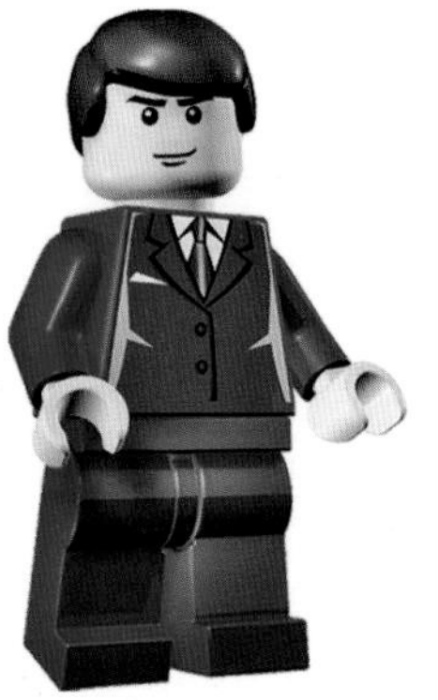

Transformation Chamber

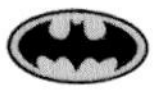

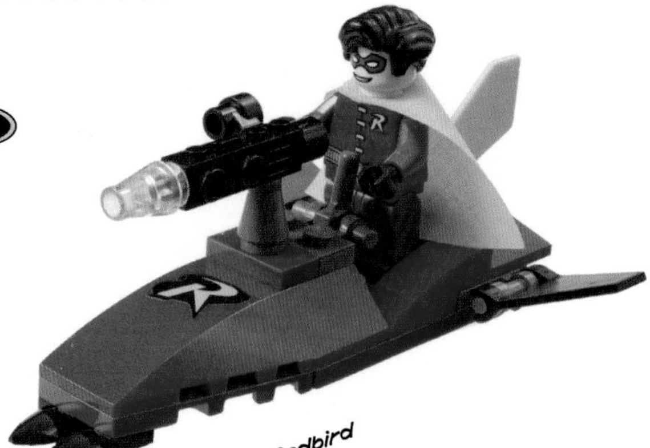

Redbird

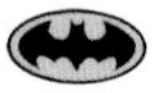

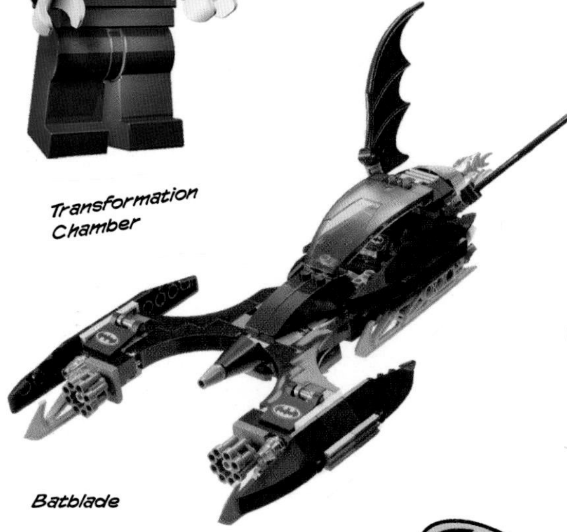

Batblade

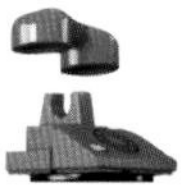

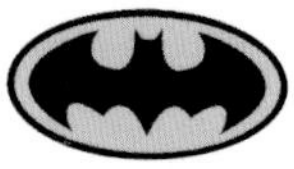

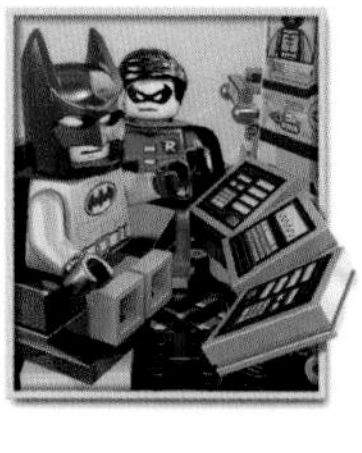

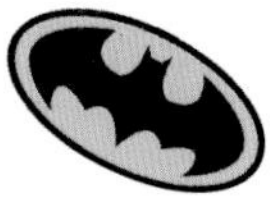

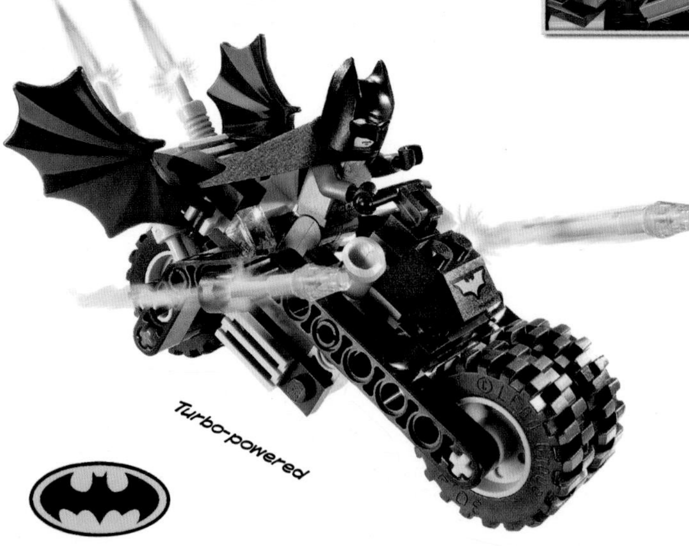

Turbo-powered

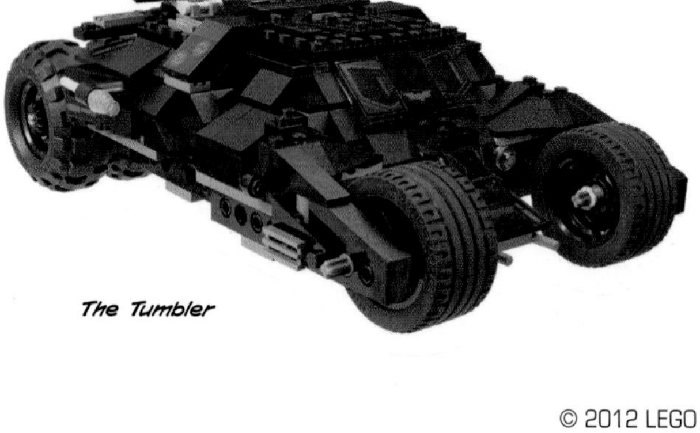

The Tumbler

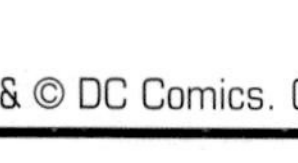

STICKERS

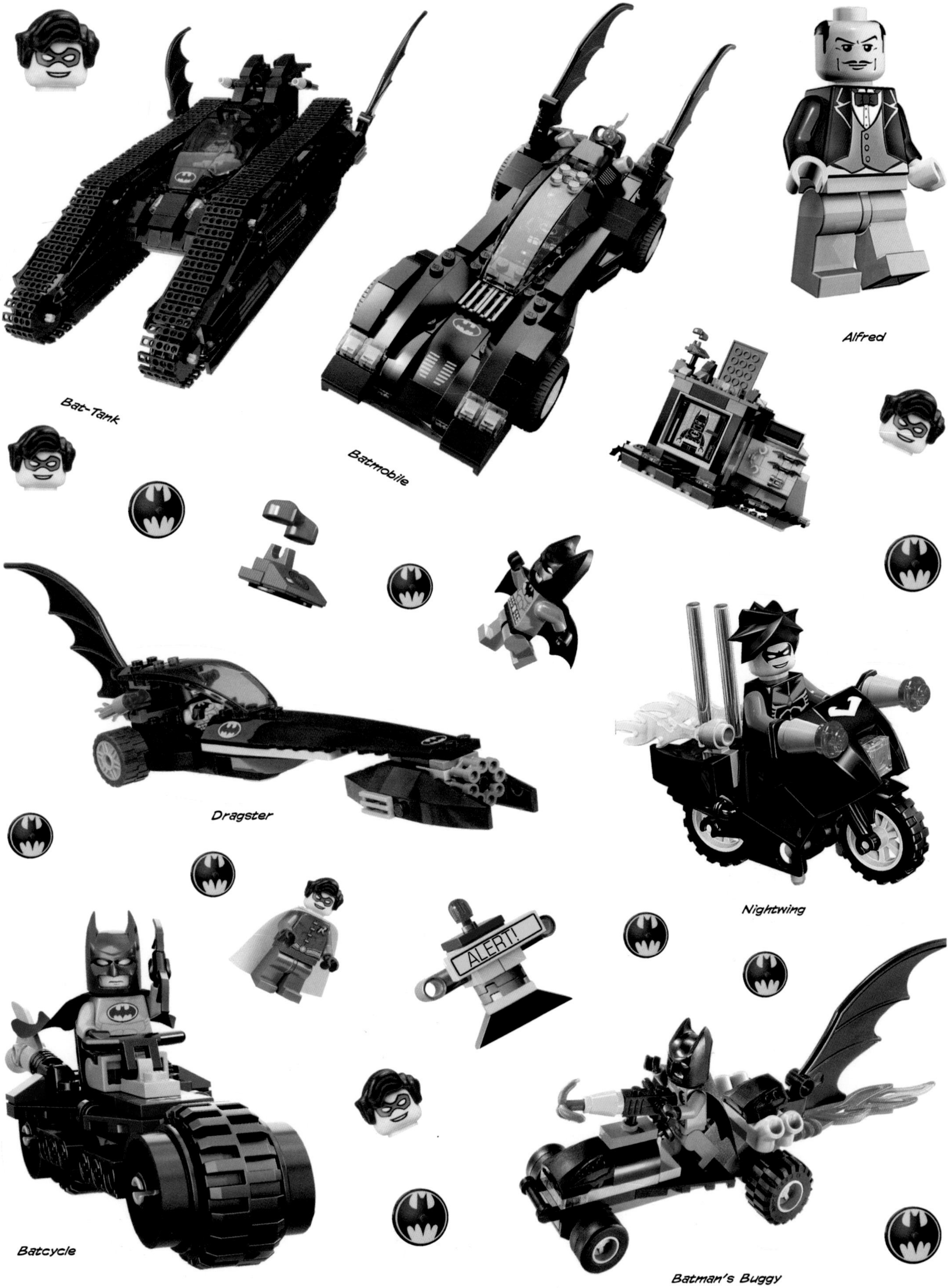
Alfred
Bat-Tank
Batmobile
Dragster
Nightwing
ALERT!
Batcycle
Batman's Buggy

STICKERS

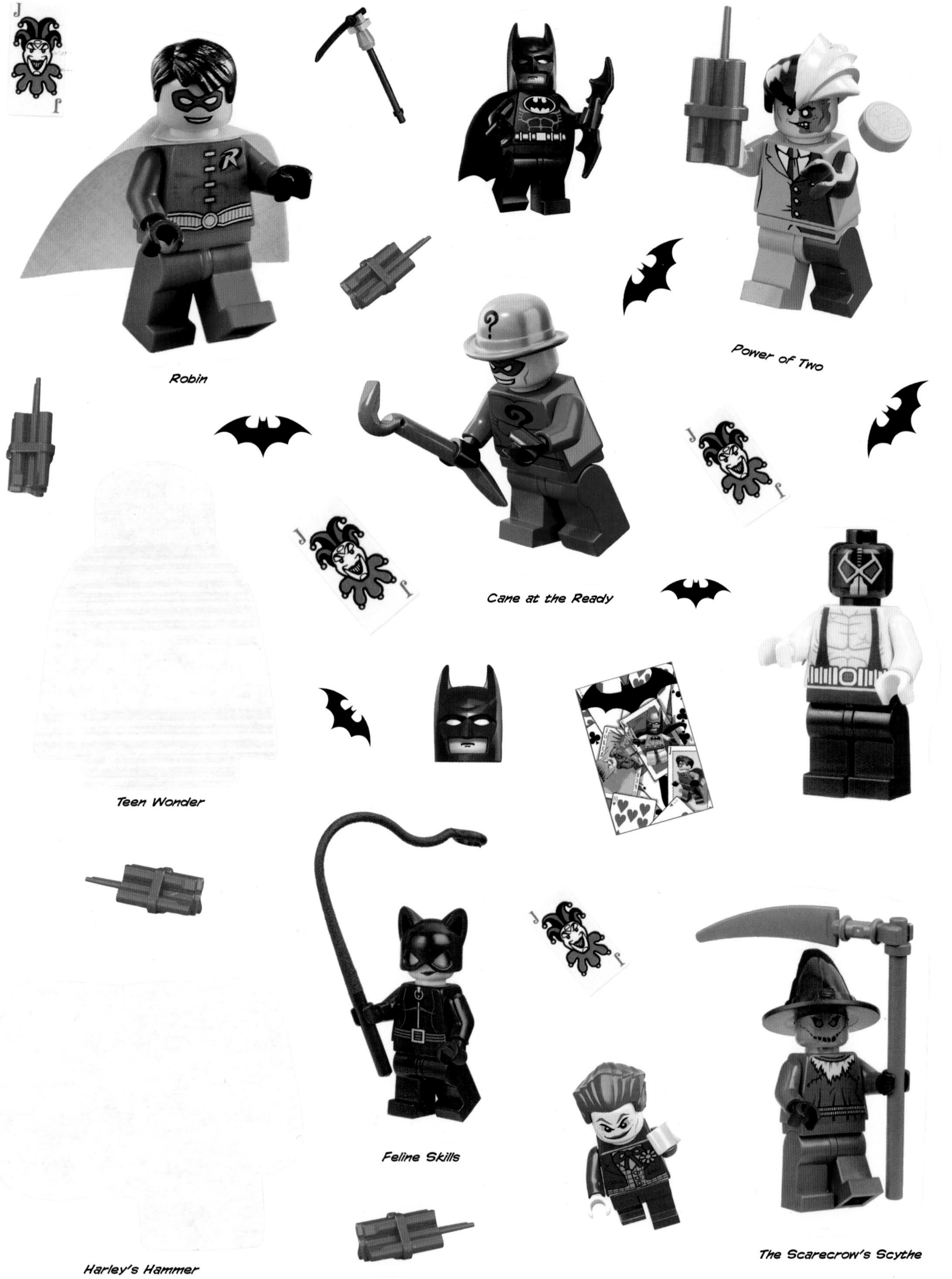
Robin
Power of Two
Cane at the Ready
Teen Wonder
Feline Skills
The Scarecrow's Scythe
Harley's Hammer

STICKERS

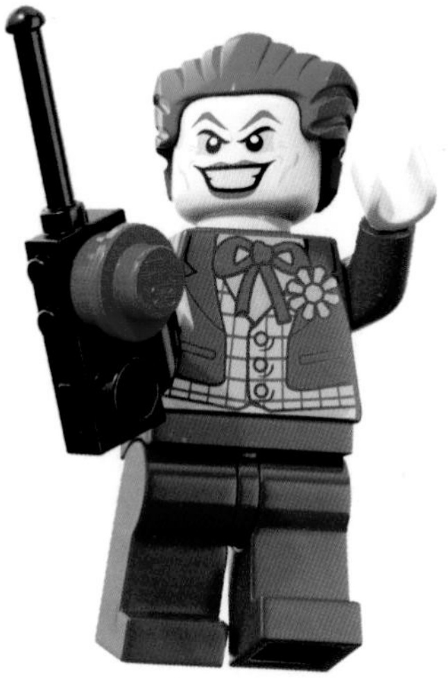

Bomb Detonator

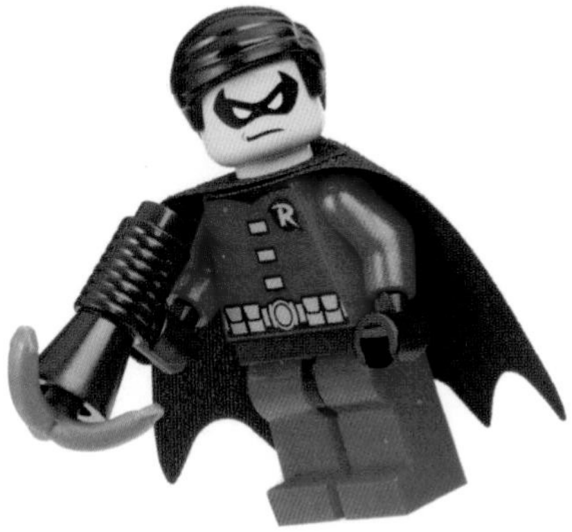

Grapnel Gun

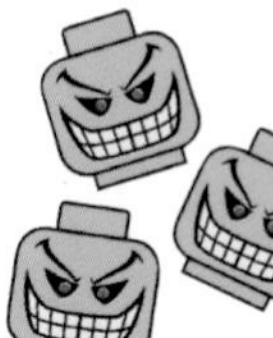

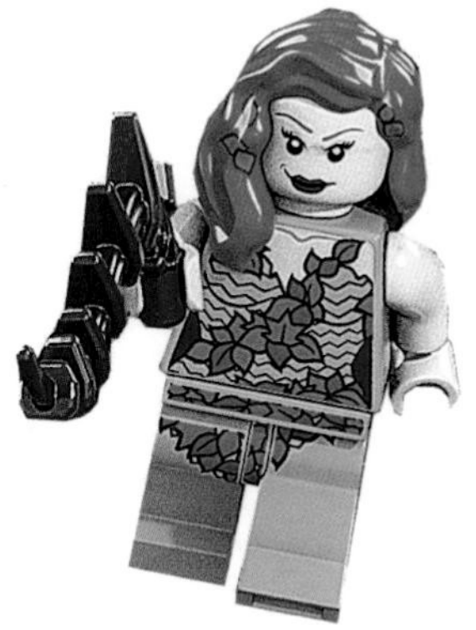

Attack of the Plants

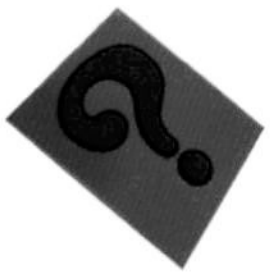

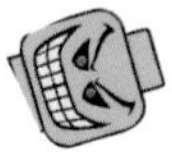

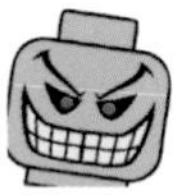

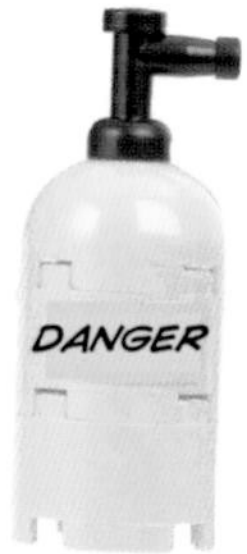
DANGER

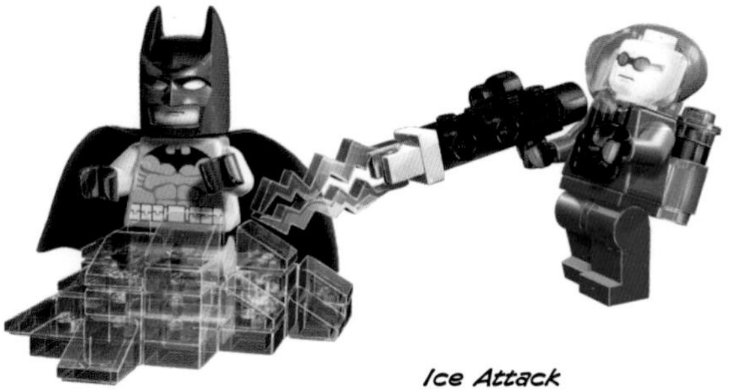

Ice Attack

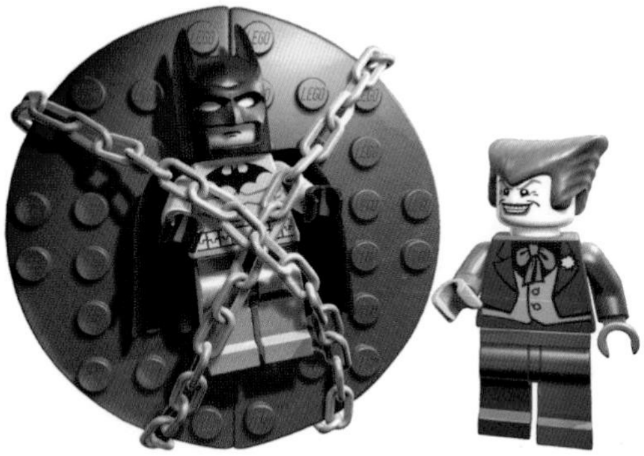

The Joker's Prisoner

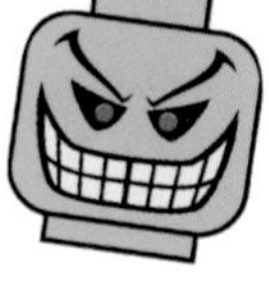

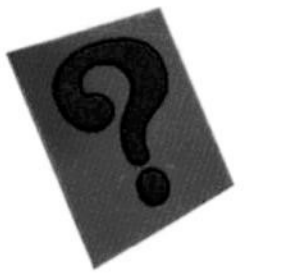

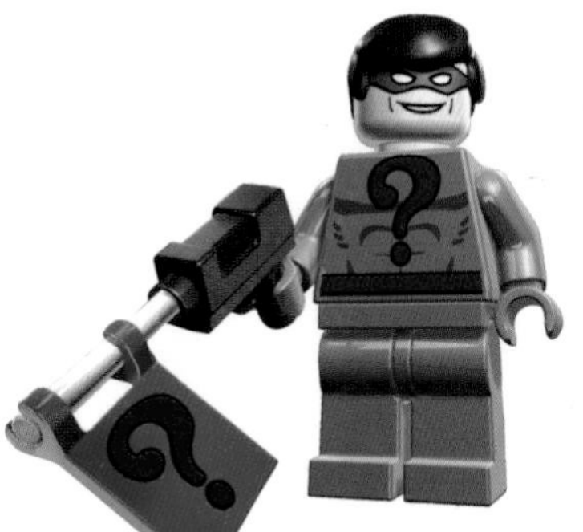

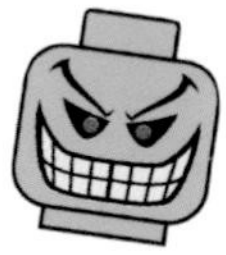

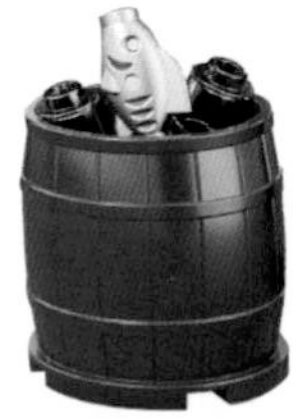

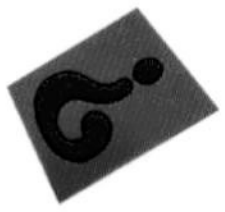

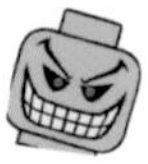

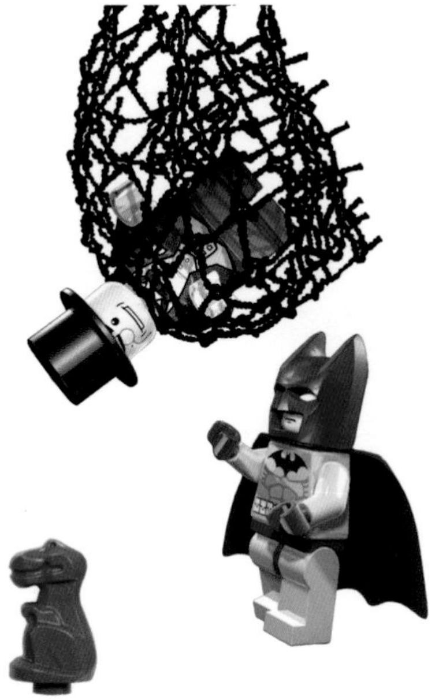

Caught in a Net

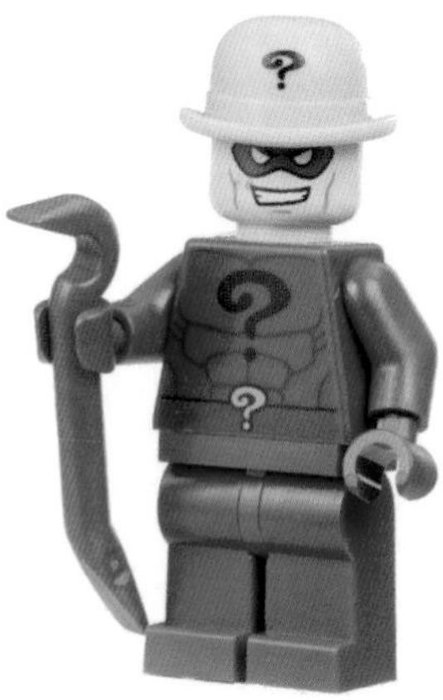

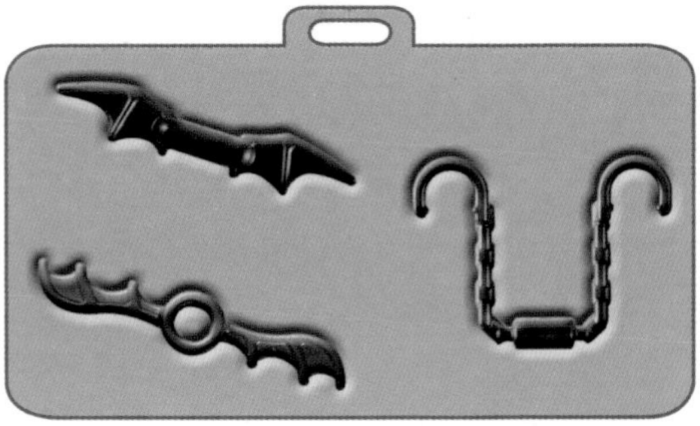

More Batarangs

STICKERS

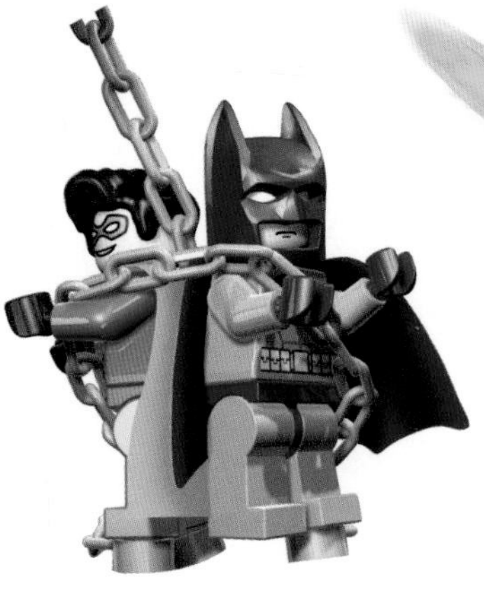

Trapped

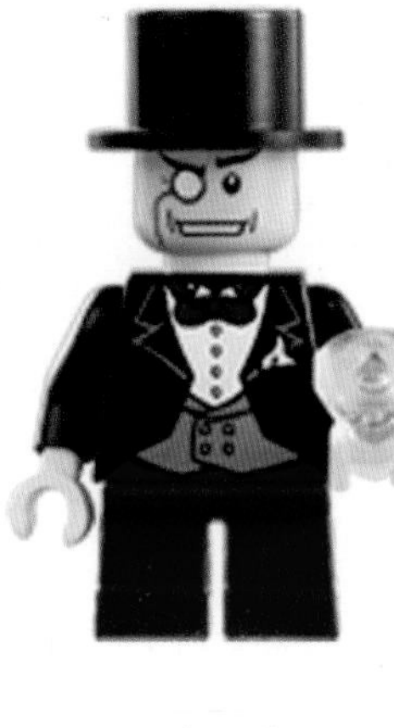

Foul Foe

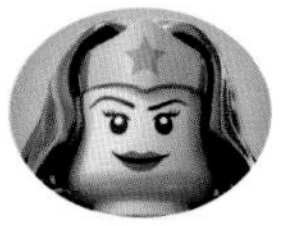

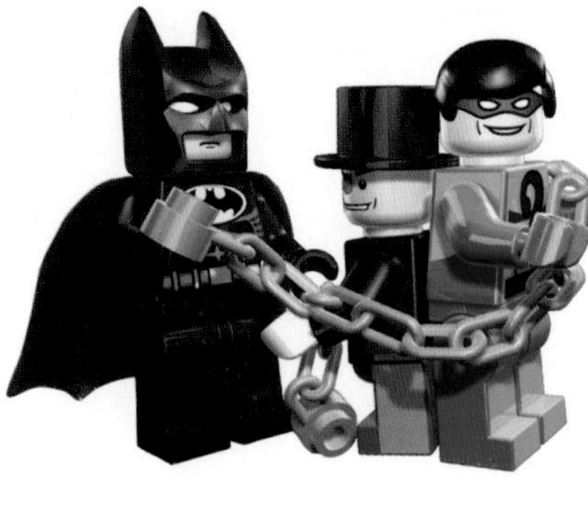

All Tied Up

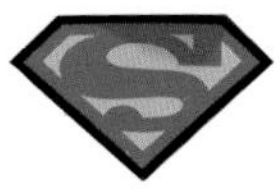

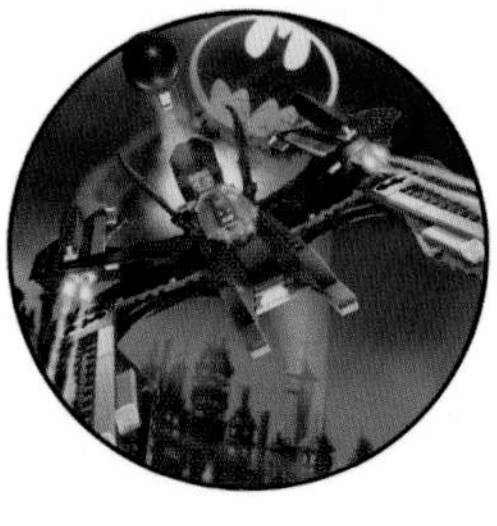

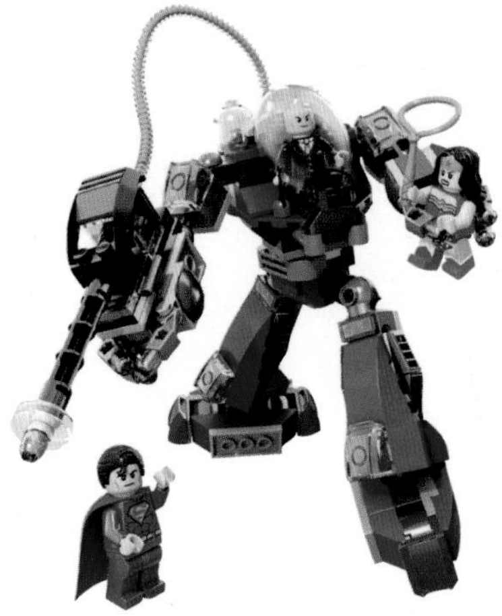

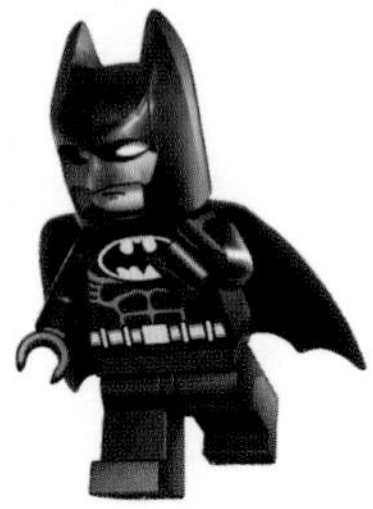

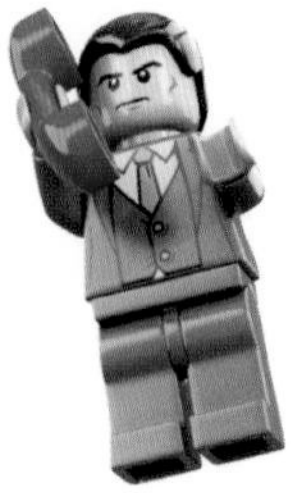

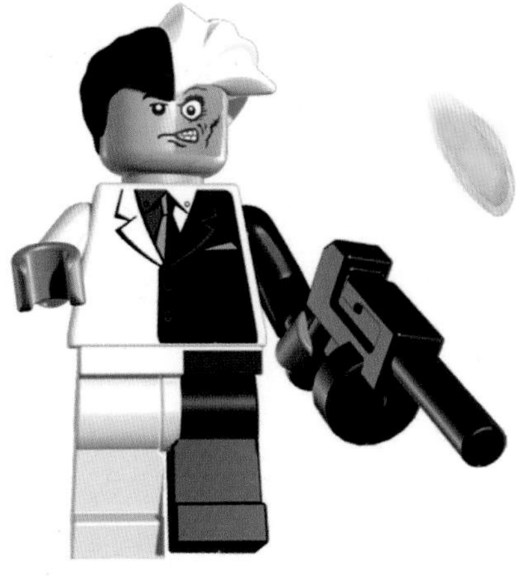

At Gunpoint

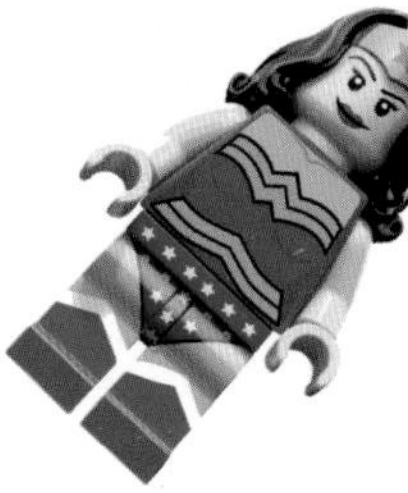

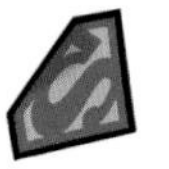

Double Trouble

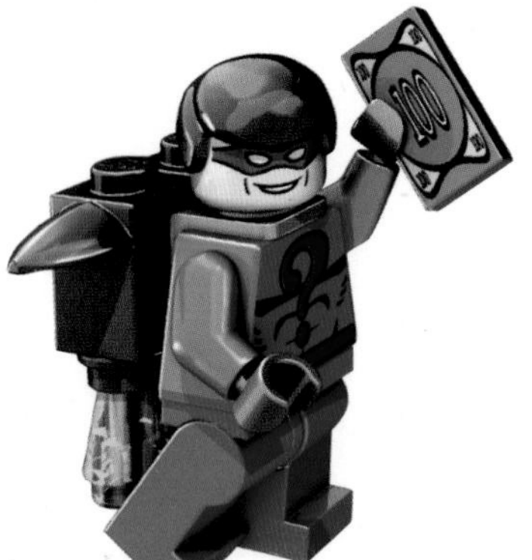

Daylight Robbery

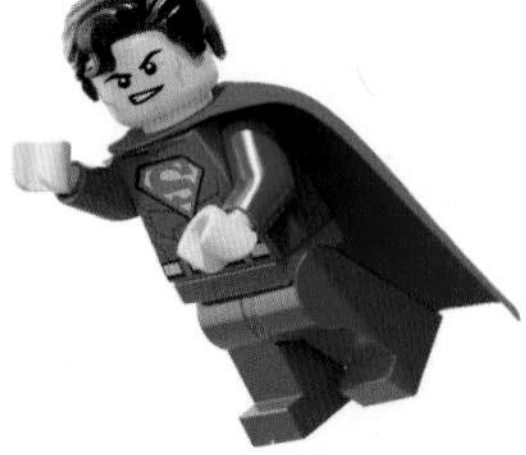

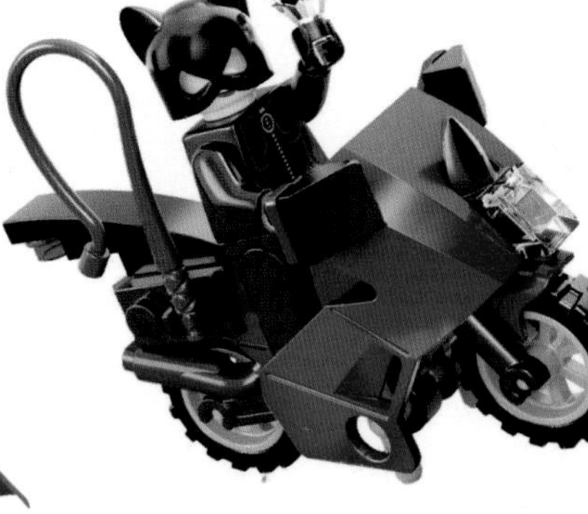

Cat-burglar

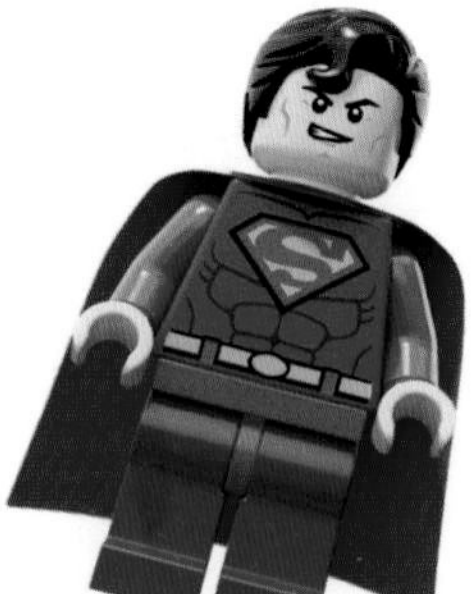

STICKERS

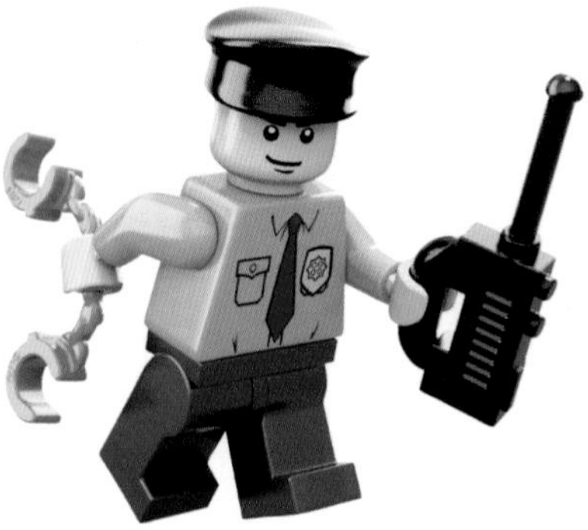
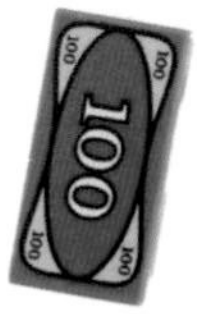
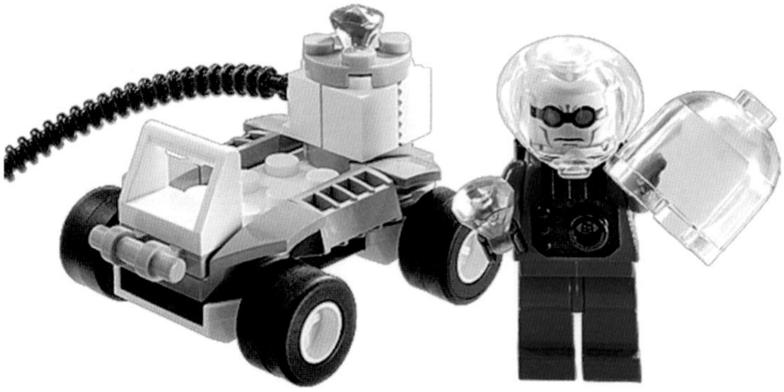
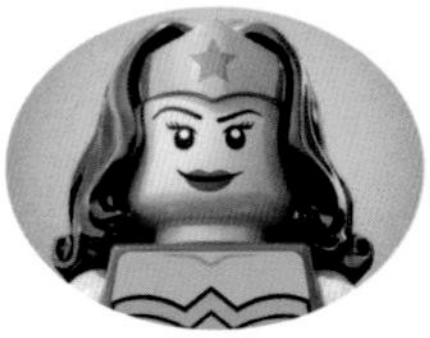

Under Arrest!

Cold as Ice

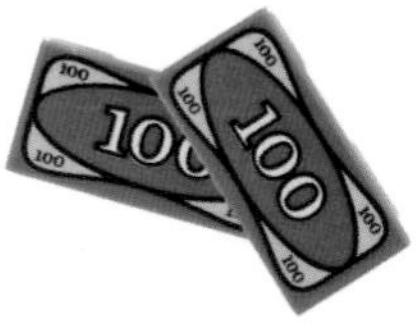
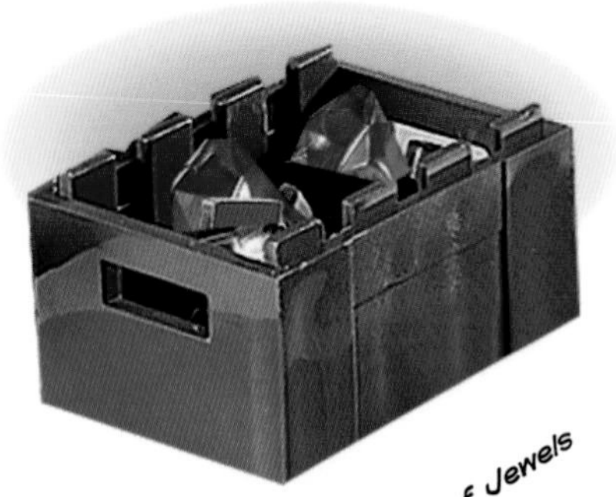
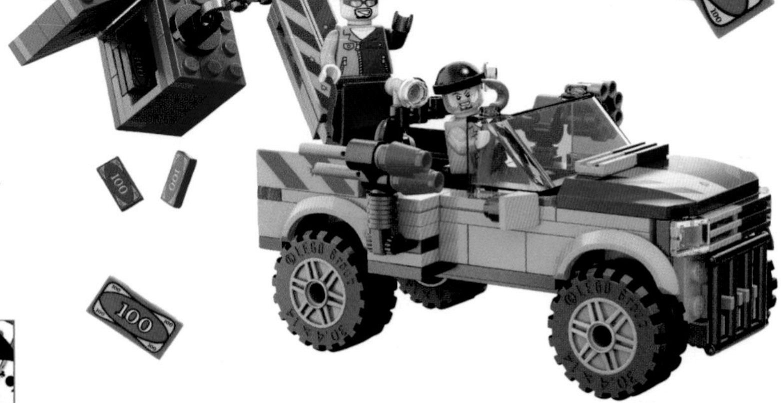
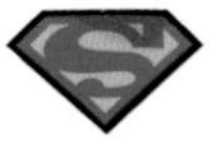

Crate of Jewels

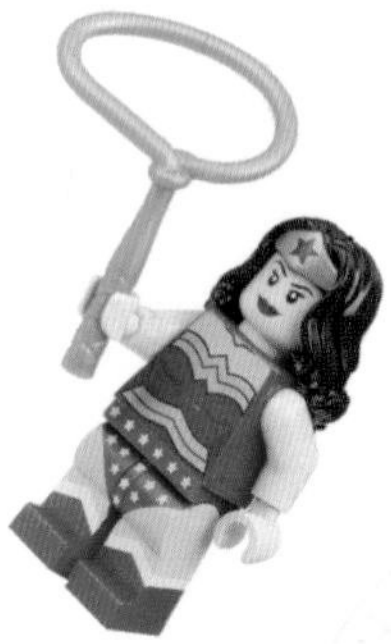
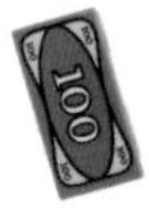
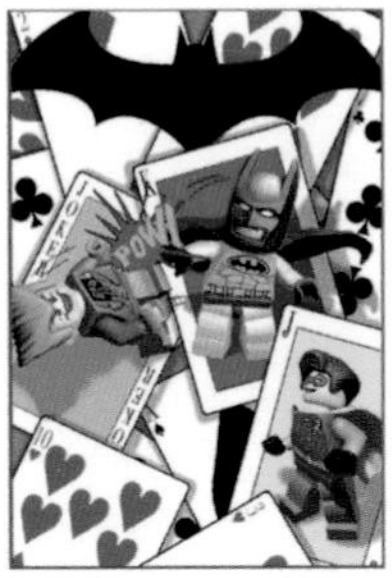

Bank Robbery

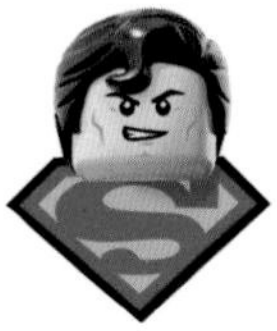
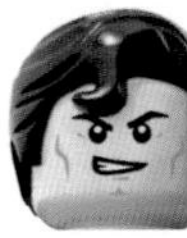

Lex Luthor

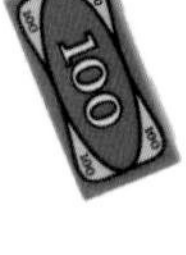
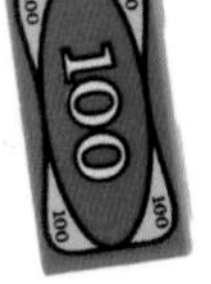
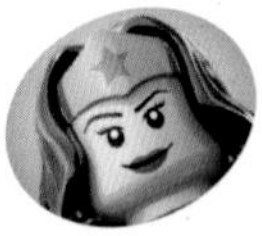

Superman

Wonder Woman

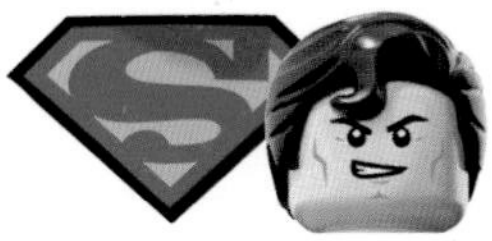
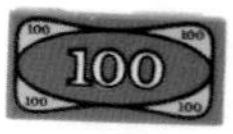
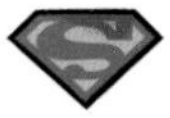

STICKERS

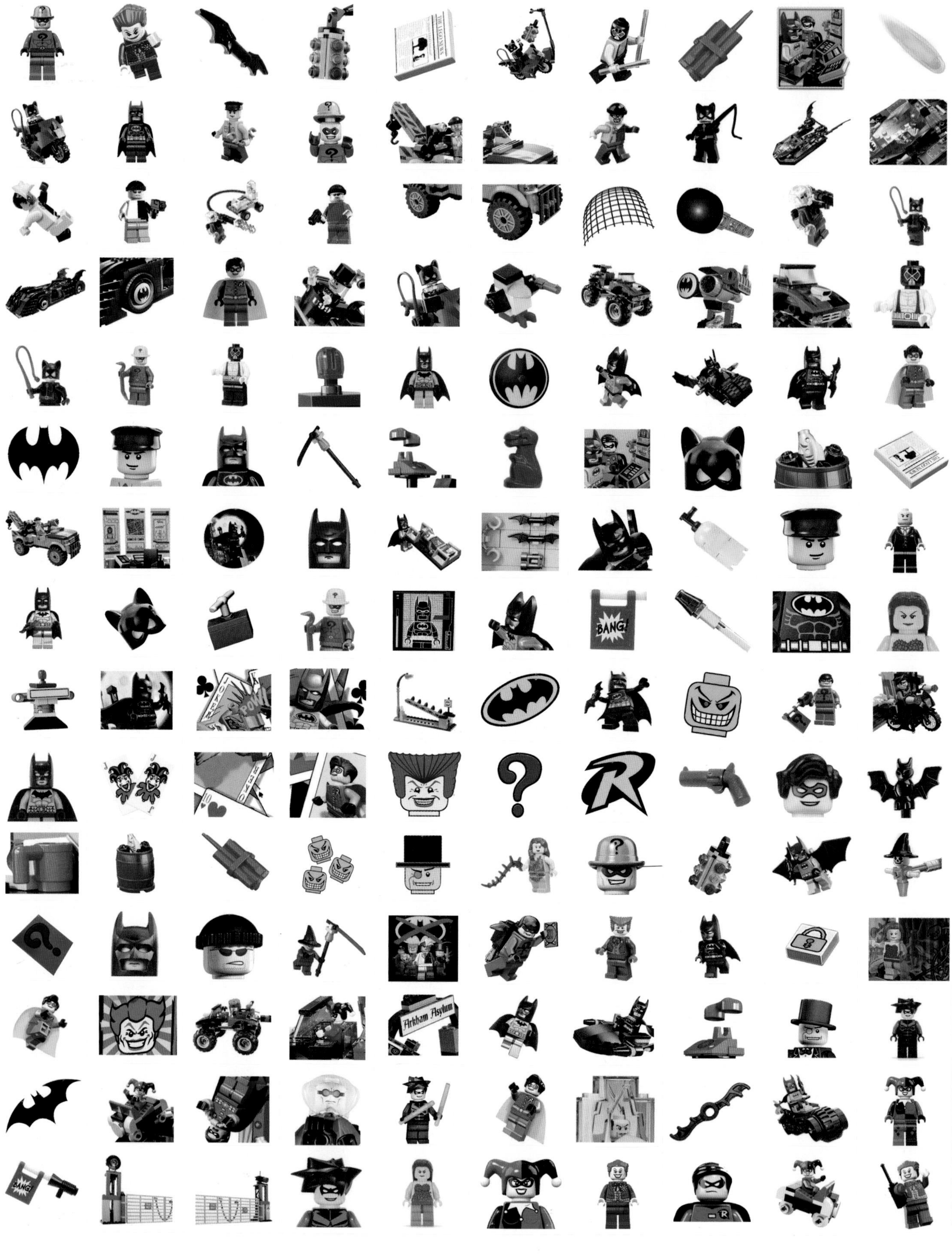
BANG!
Arkham Asylum

STICKERS

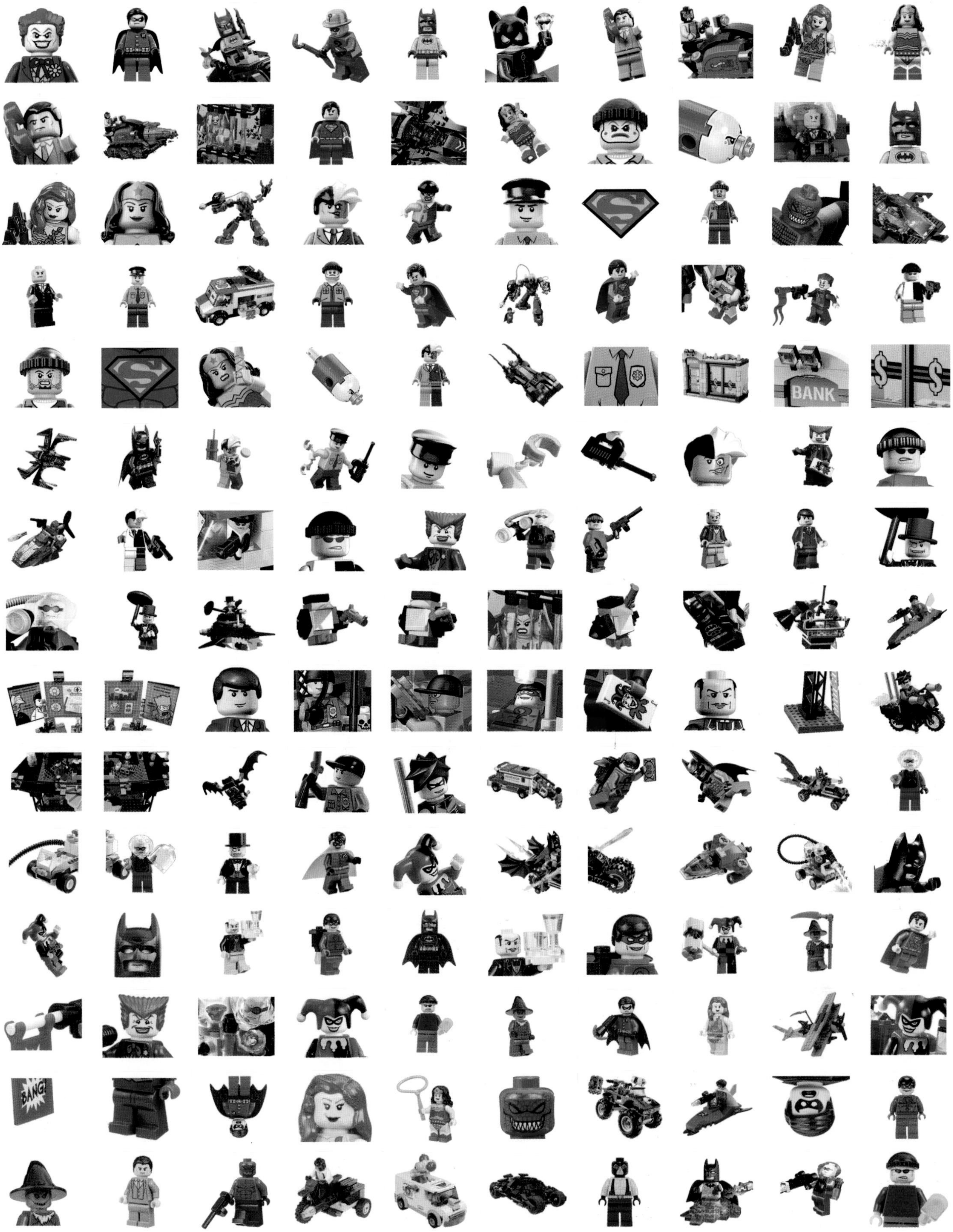
BANK
BANG!

EXTRA STICKERS

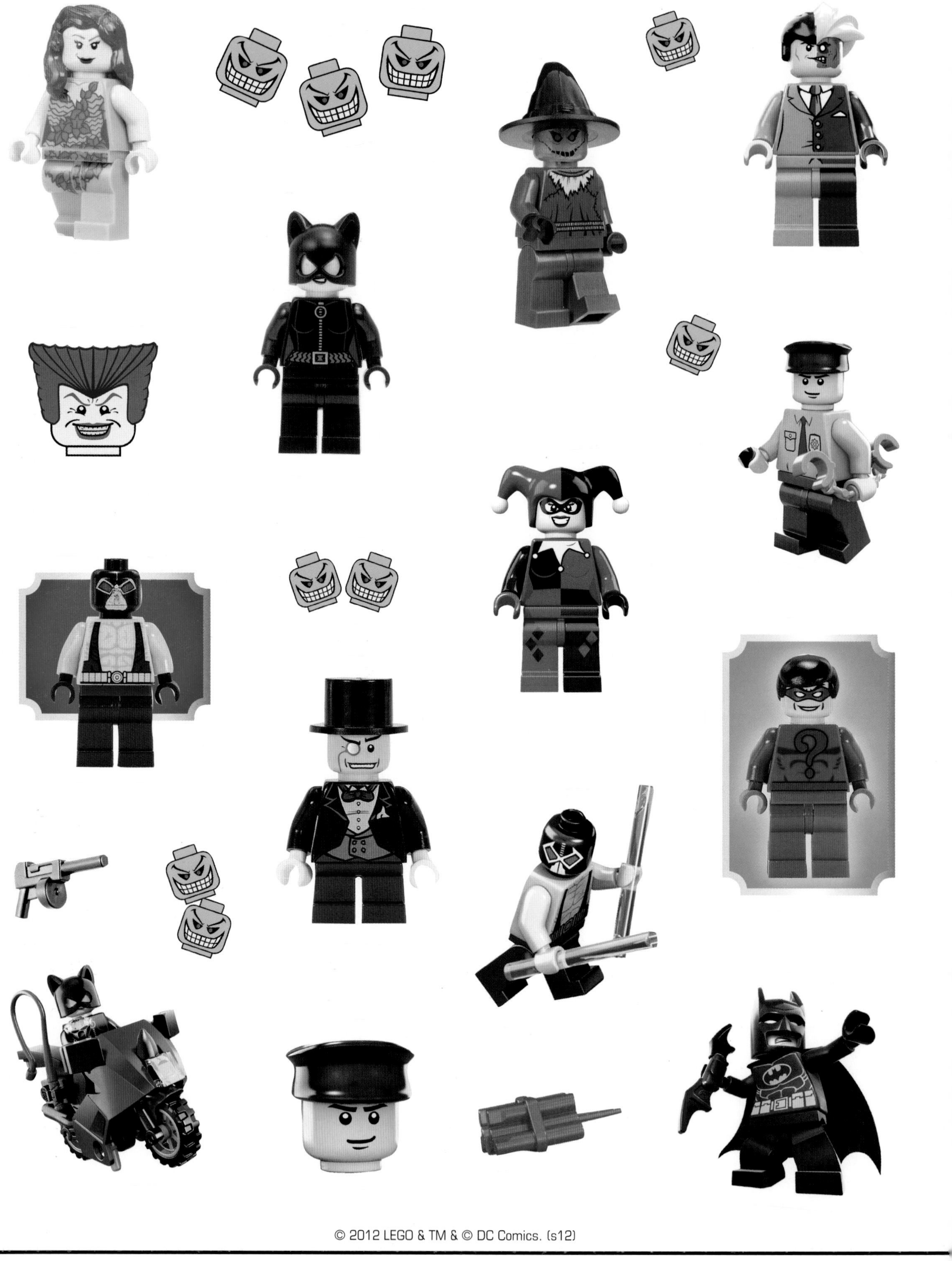

EXTRA STICKERS

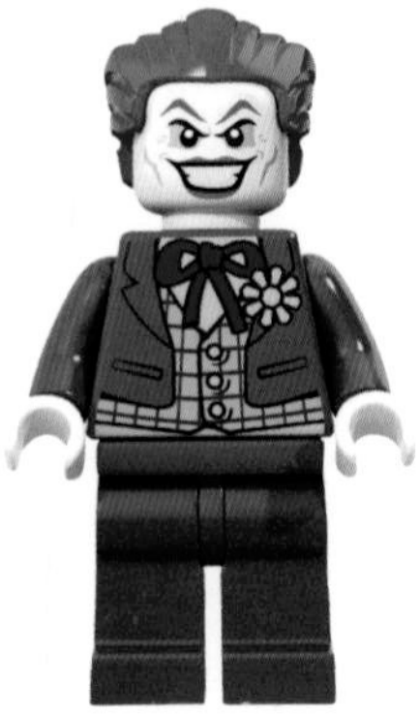
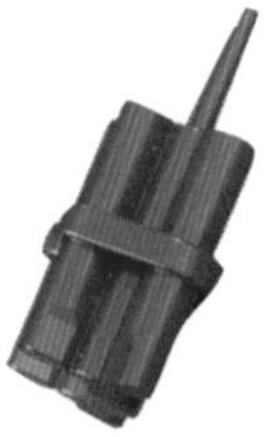
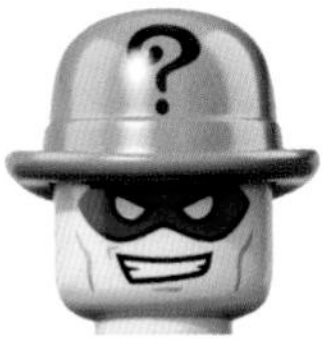
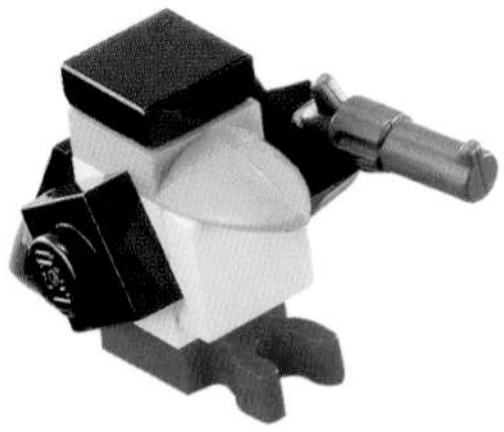
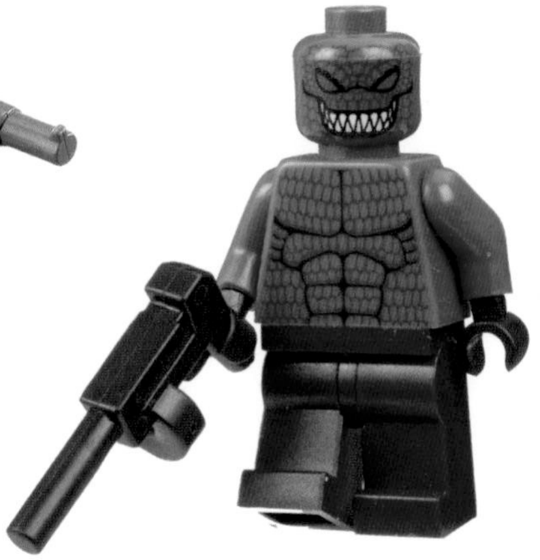
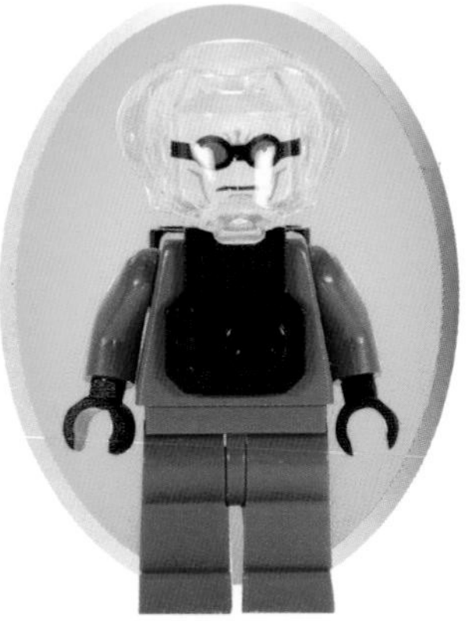
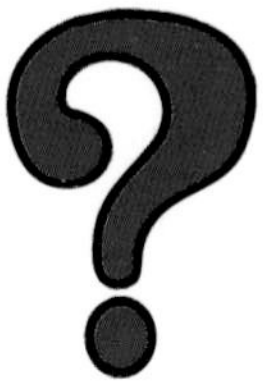
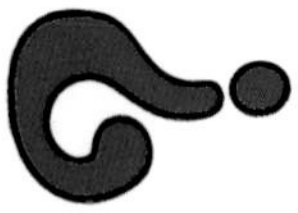
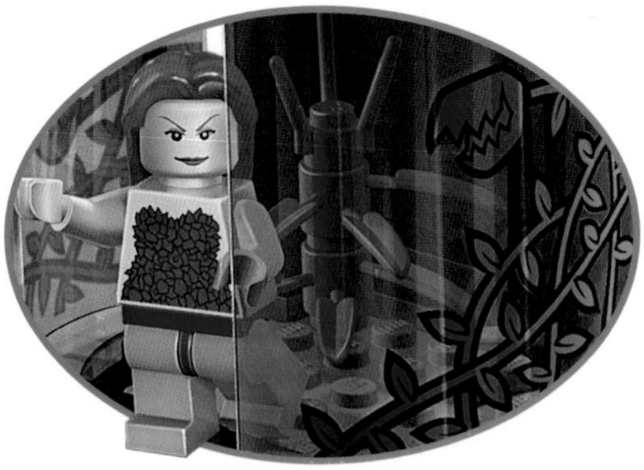
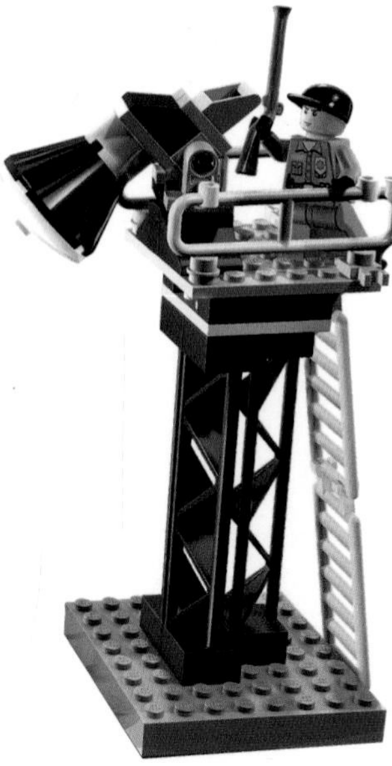
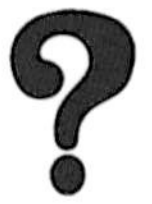
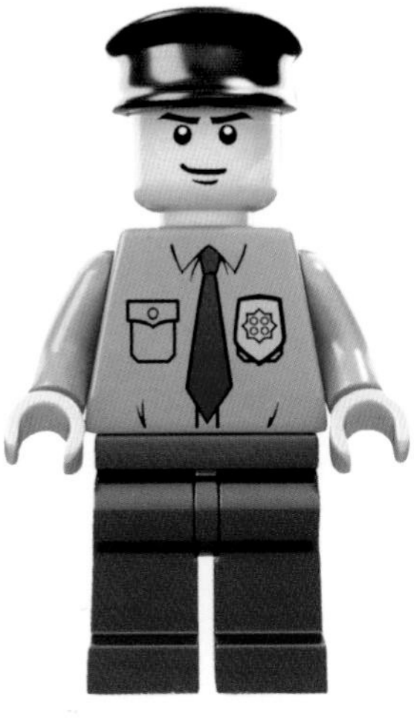
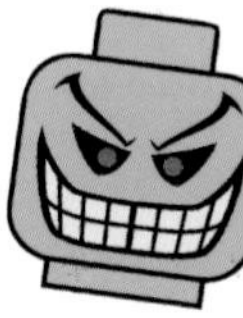
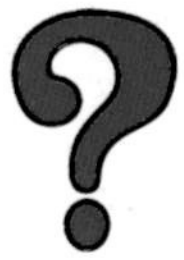
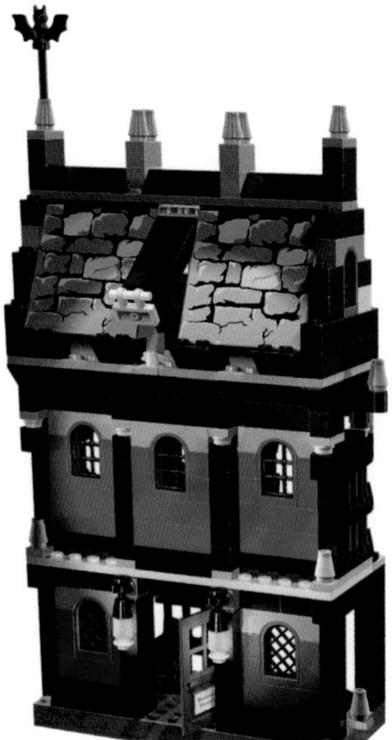
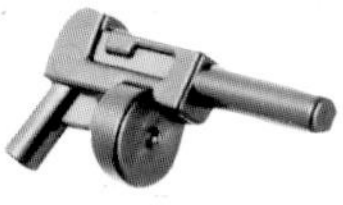
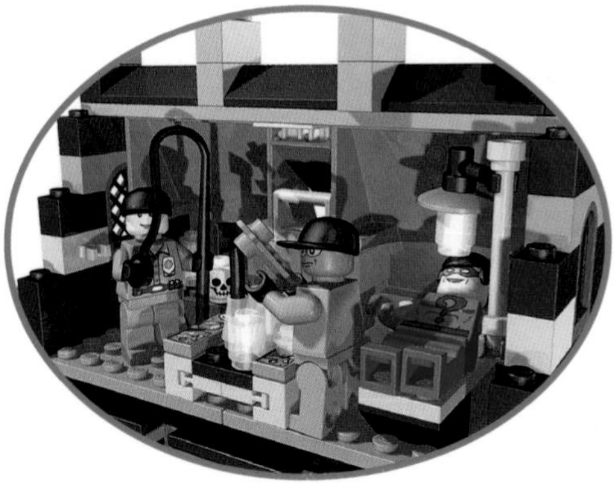
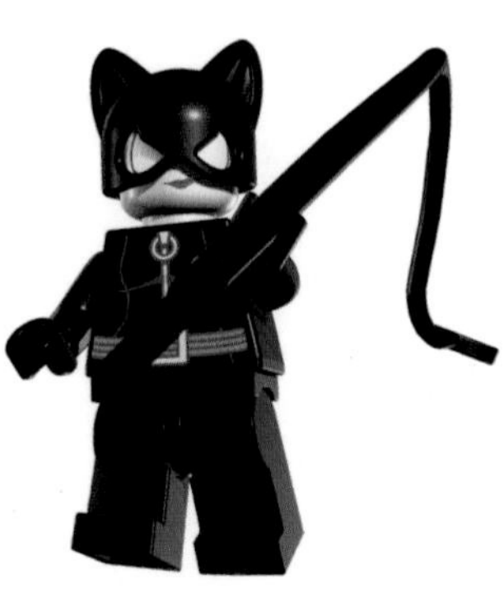

EXTRA STICKERS

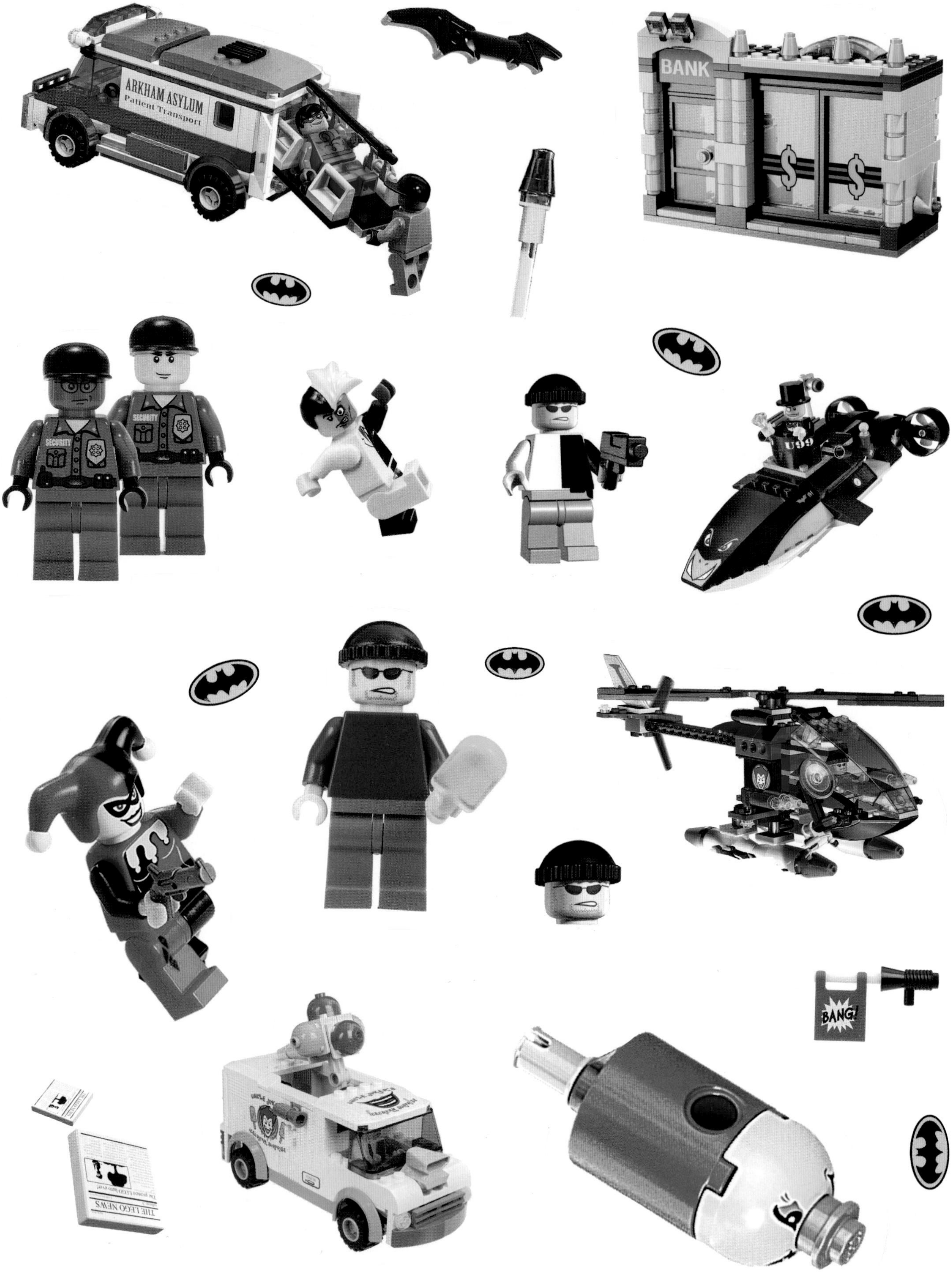
ARKHAM ASYLUM
Patient Transport
BANK
SECURITY
SECURITY
U99
BANG!
THE LEGO NEWS

EXTRA STICKERS

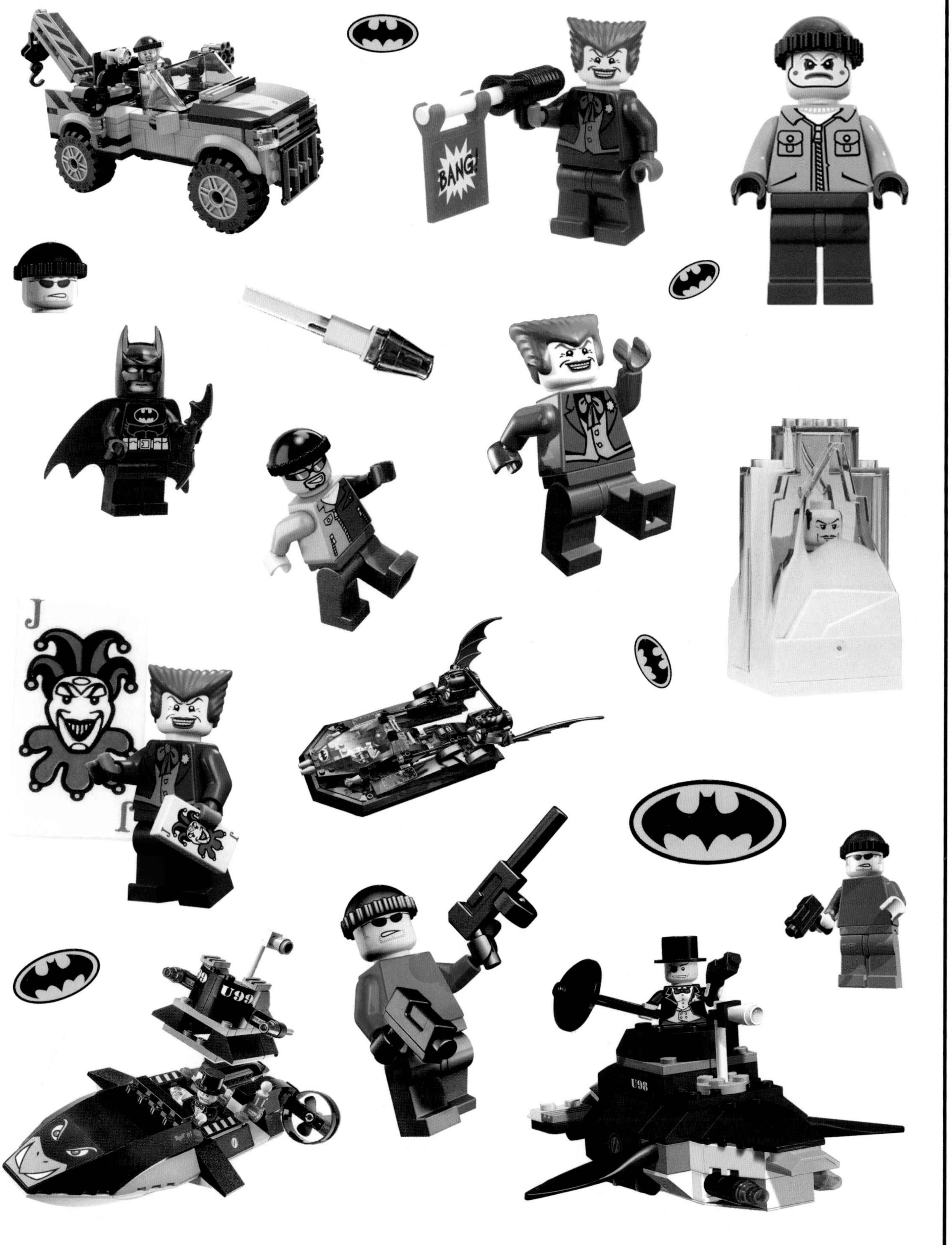
BANG!
J
U99
U98

EXTRA STICKERS

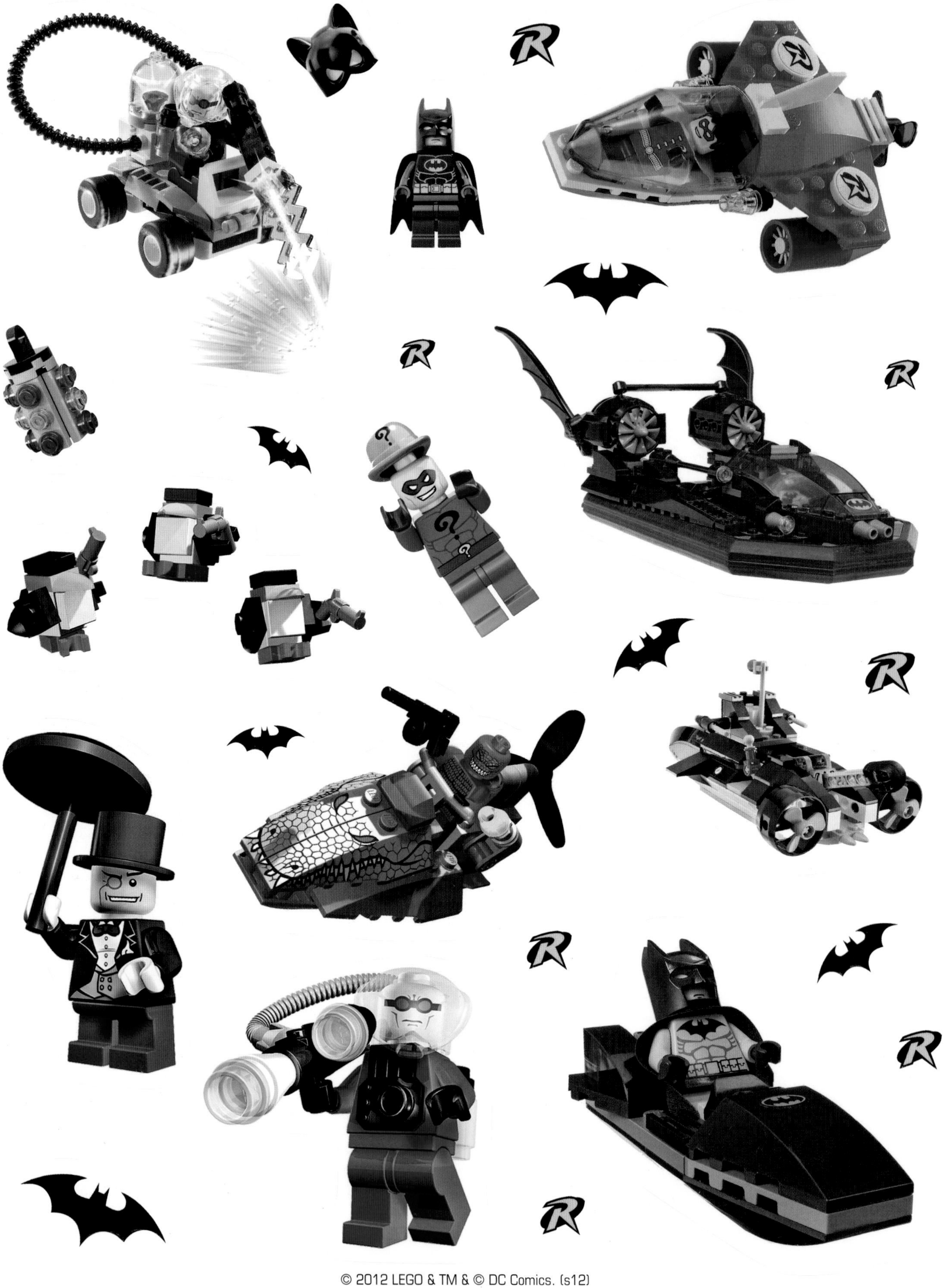

EXTRA STICKERS

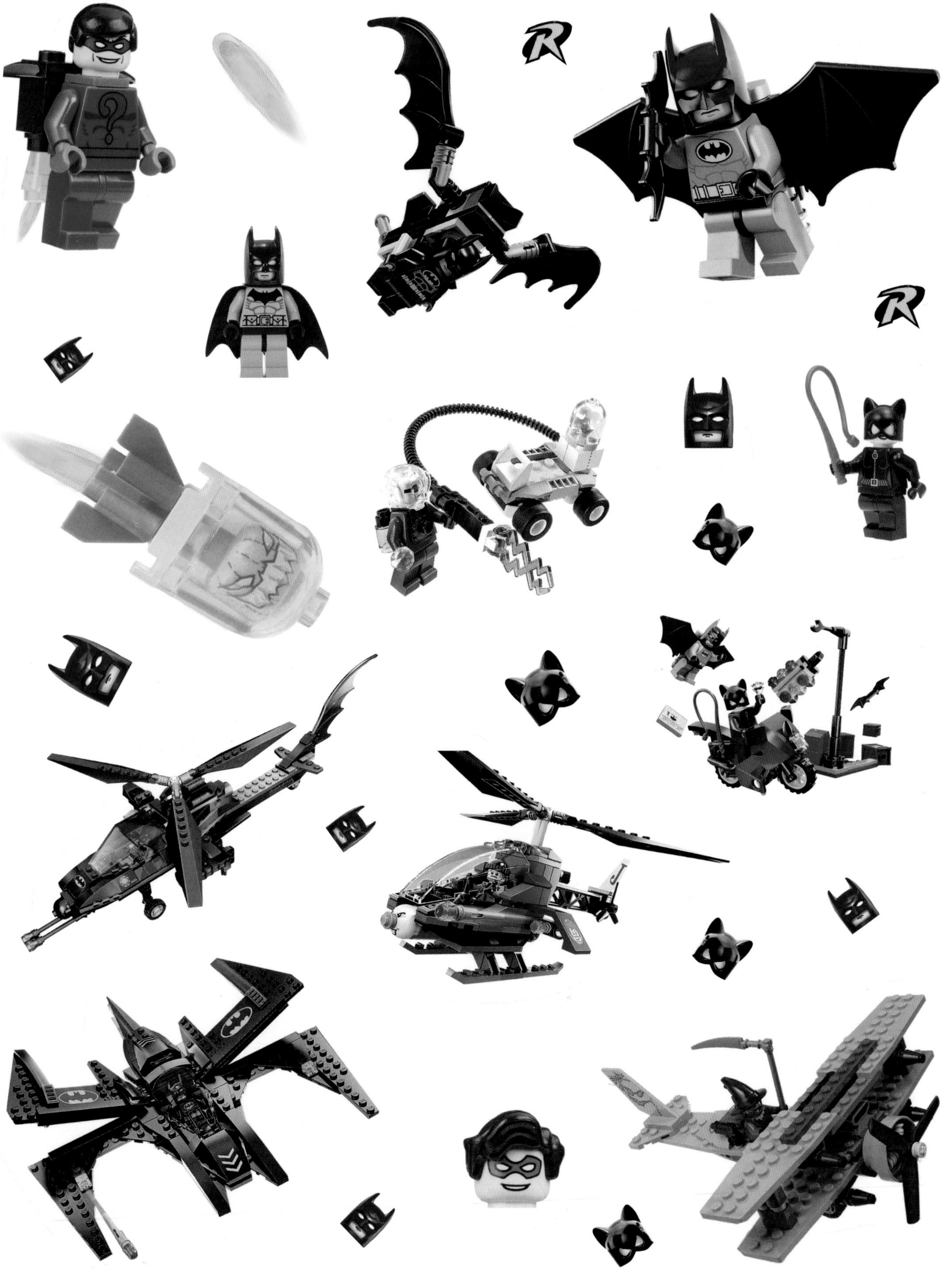

EXTRA STICKERS

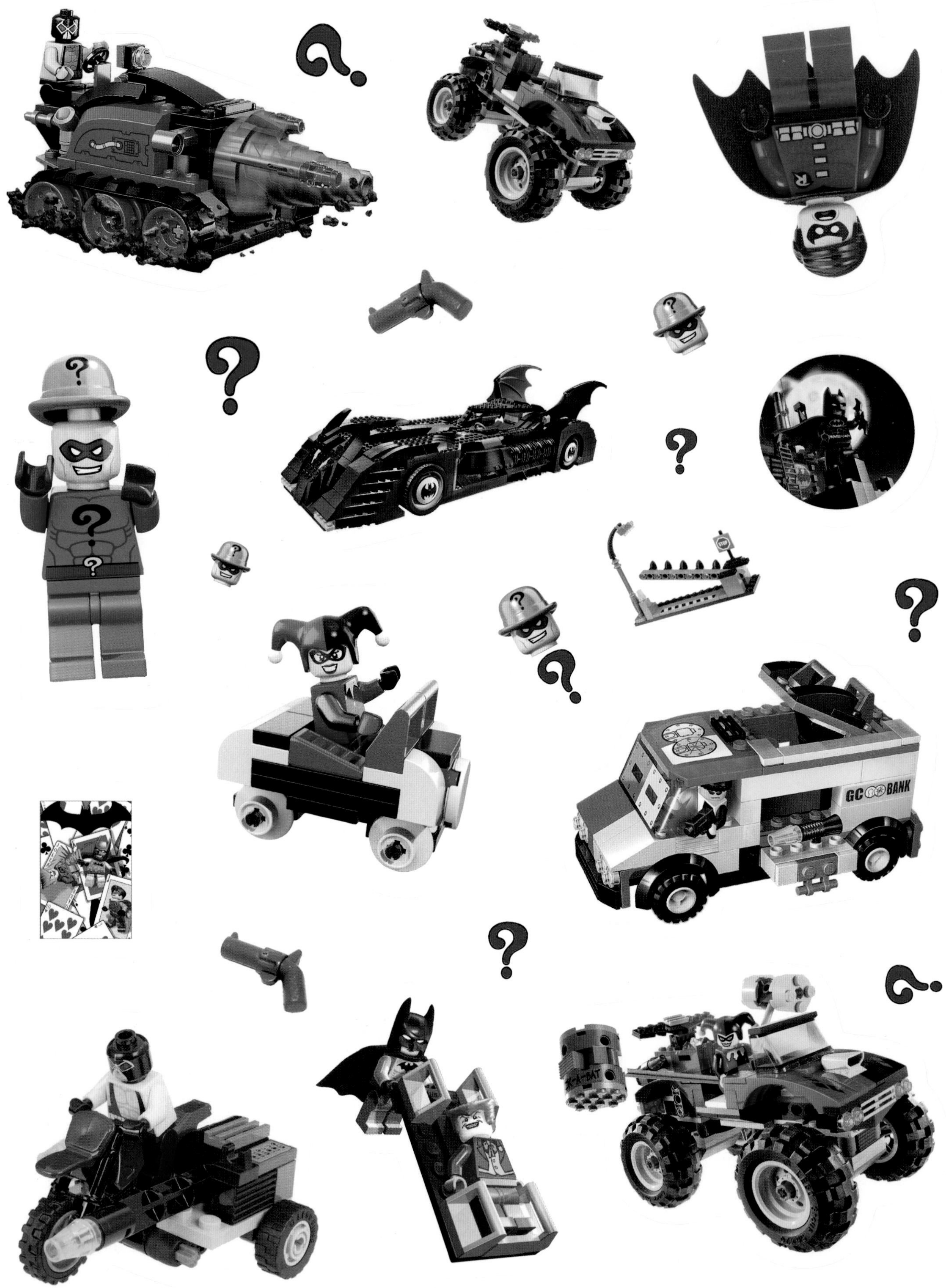
GC BANK

EXTRA STICKERS

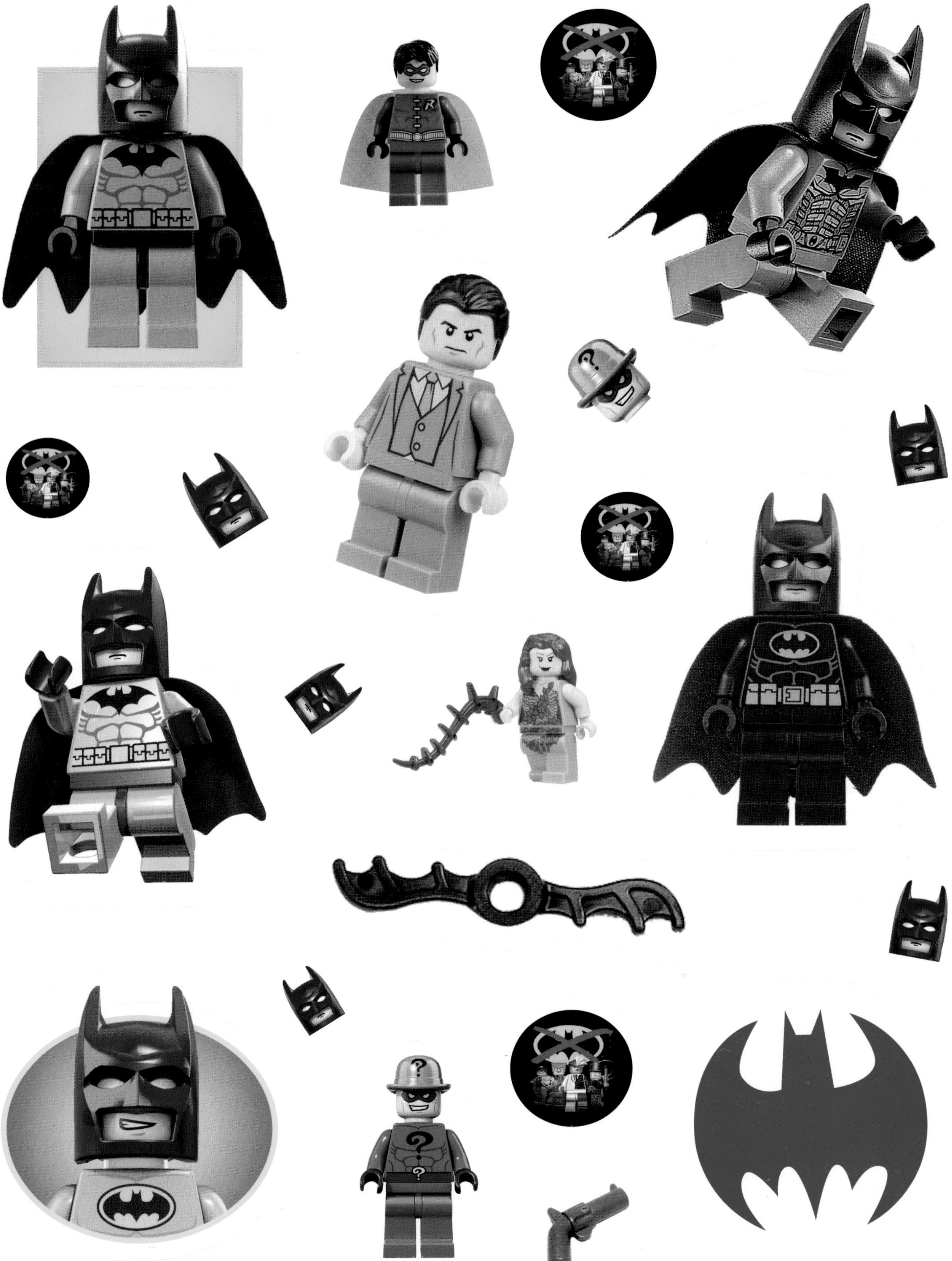

EXTRA STICKERS

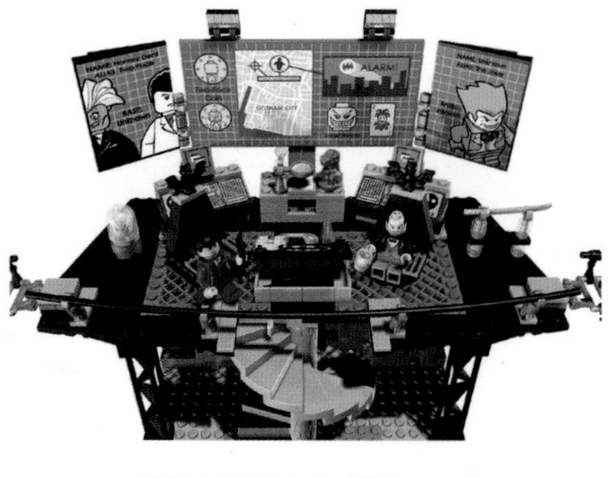
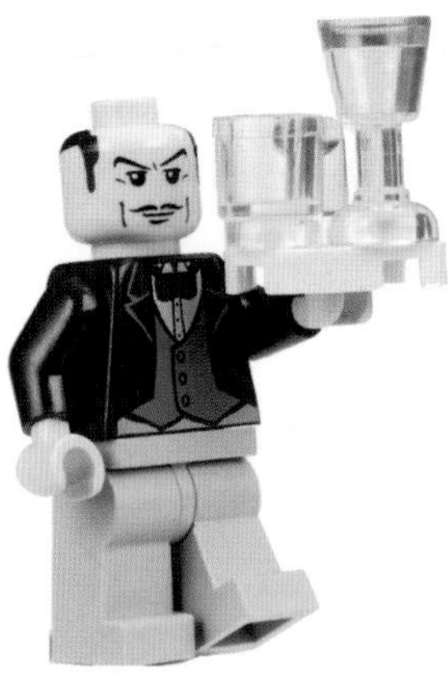
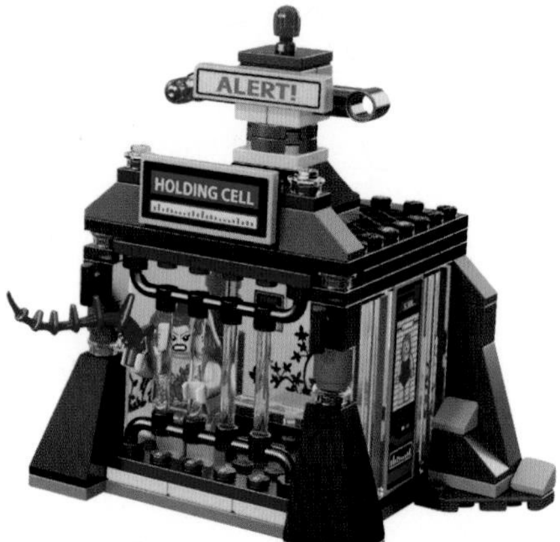
ALERT!
HOLDING CELL
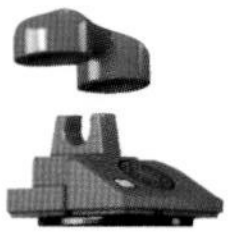
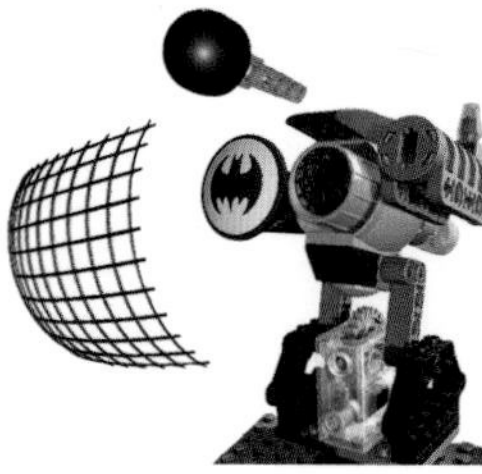
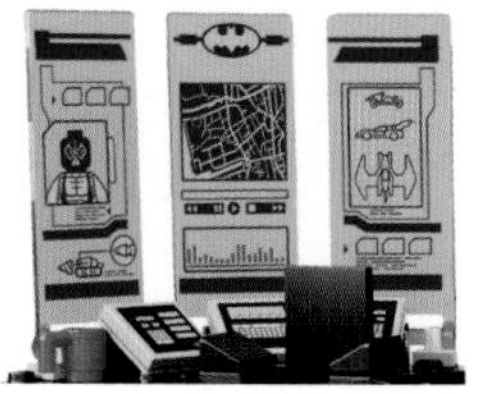
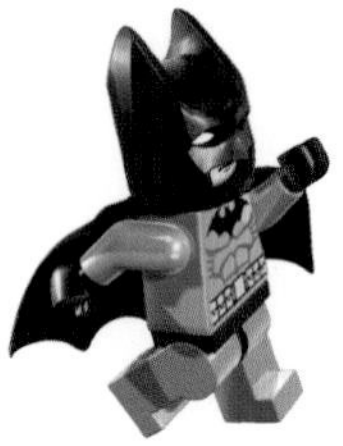
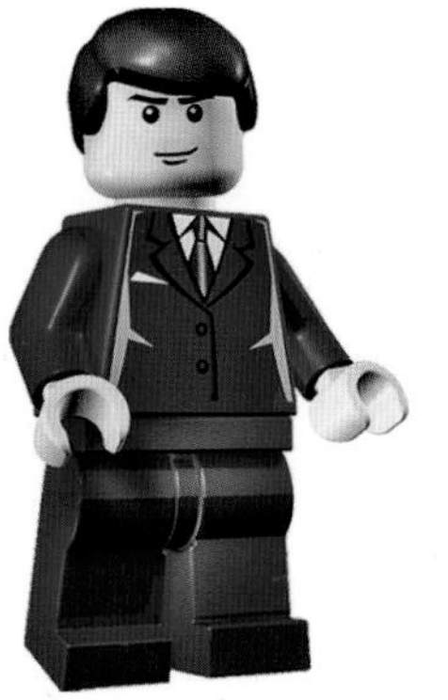
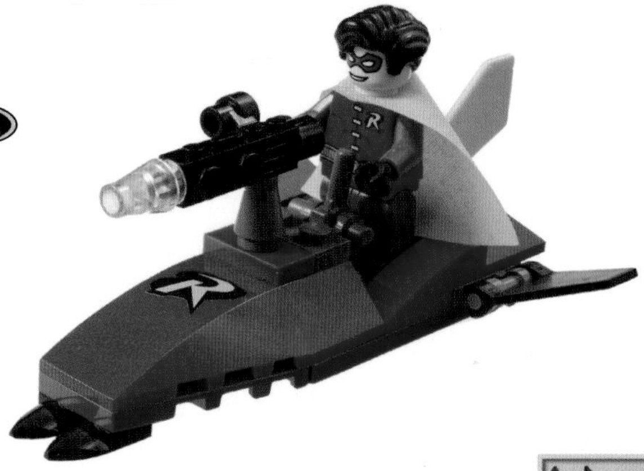
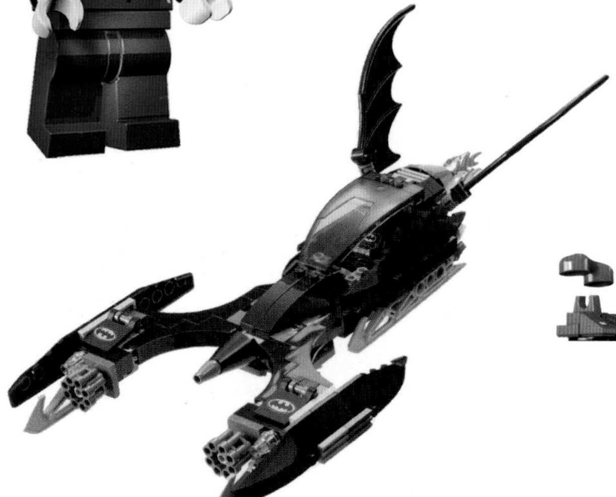
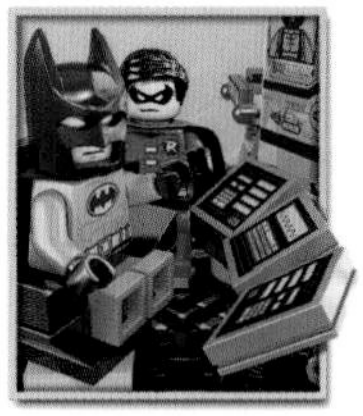
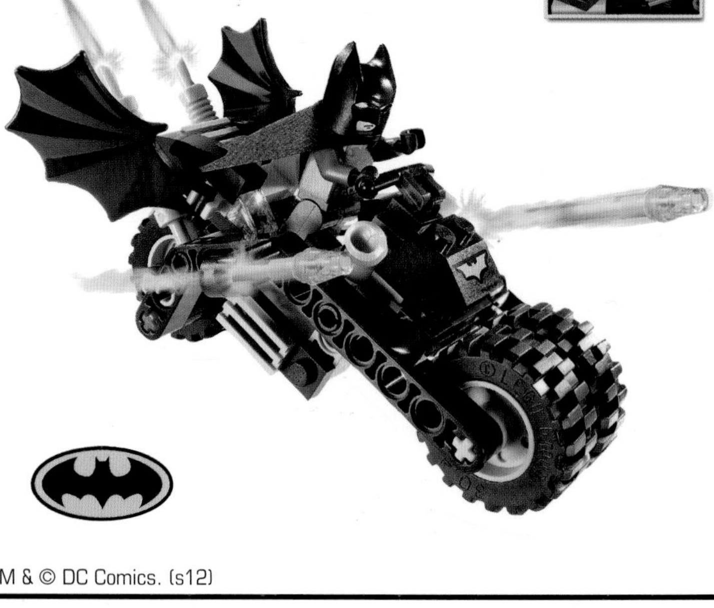
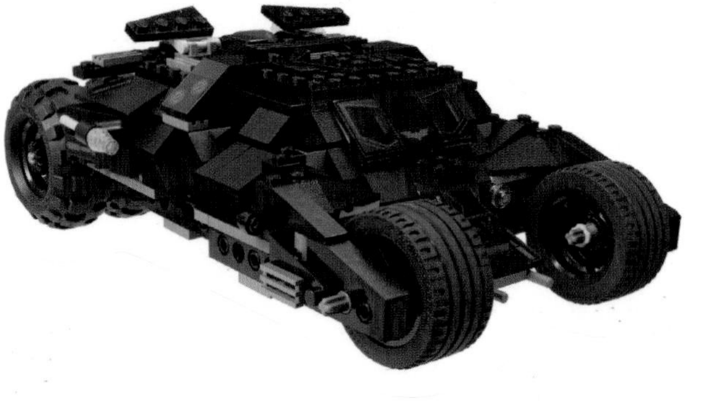

EXTRA STICKERS

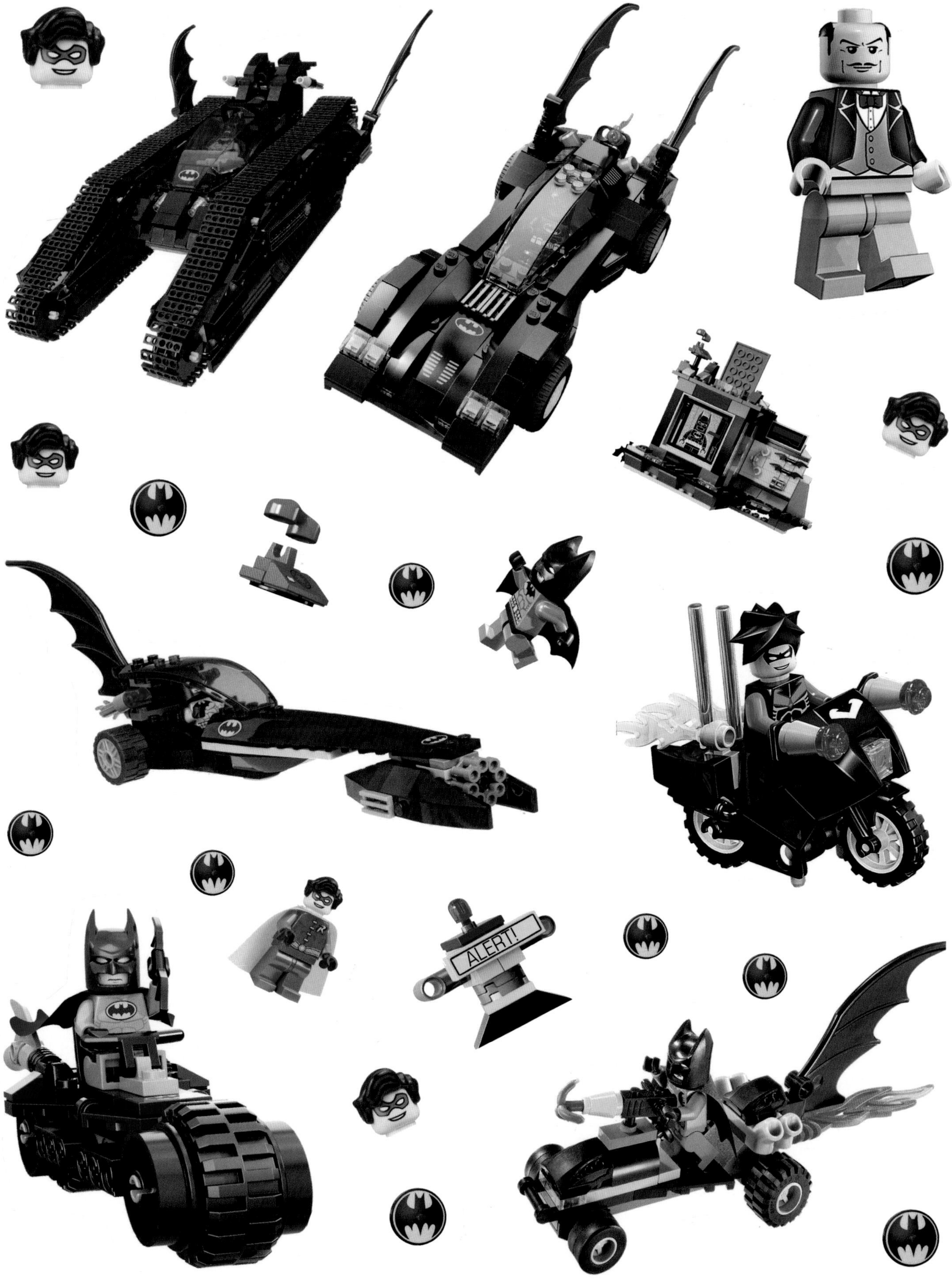
ALERT!

EXTRA STICKERS

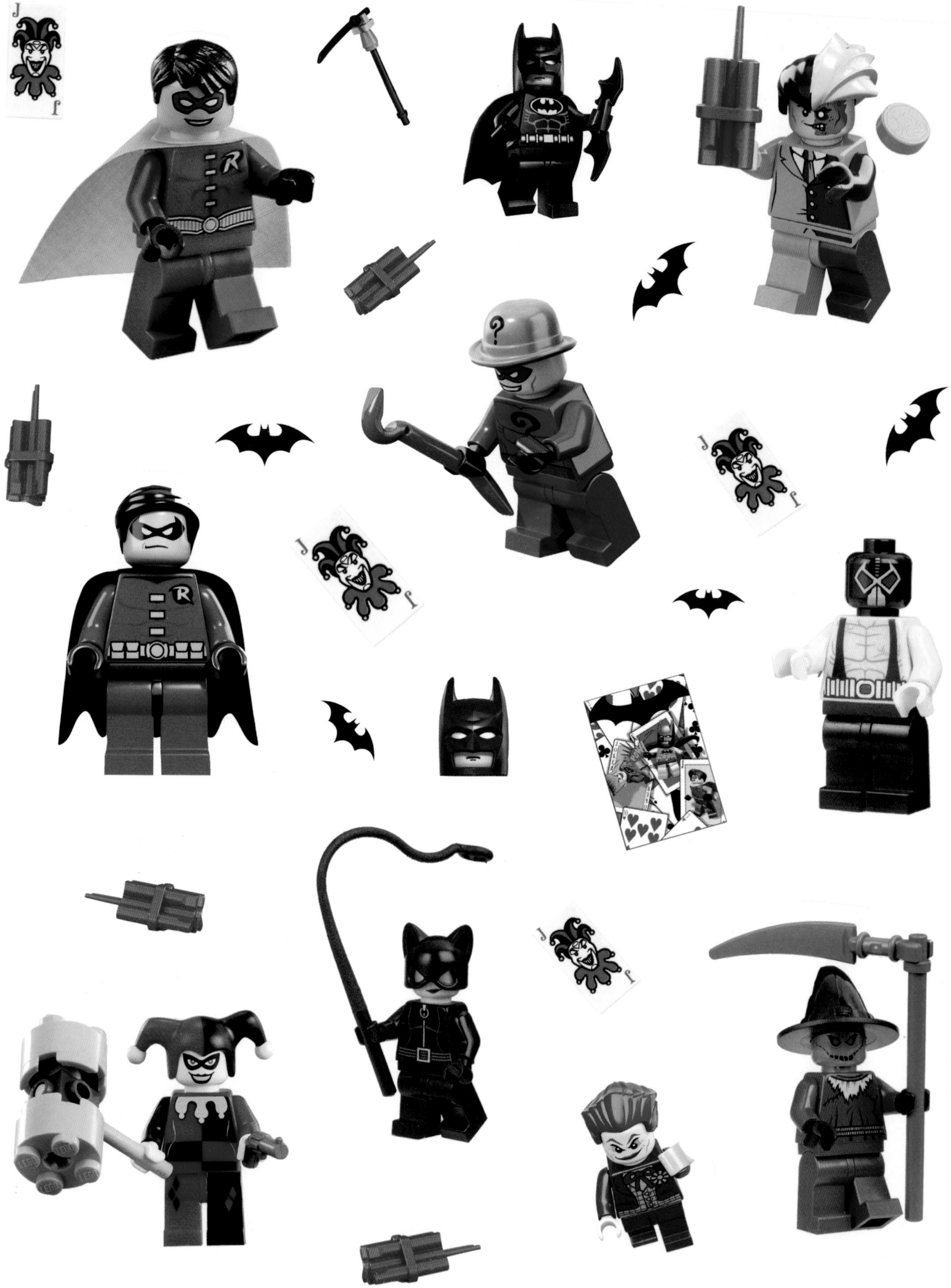

EXTRA STICKERS

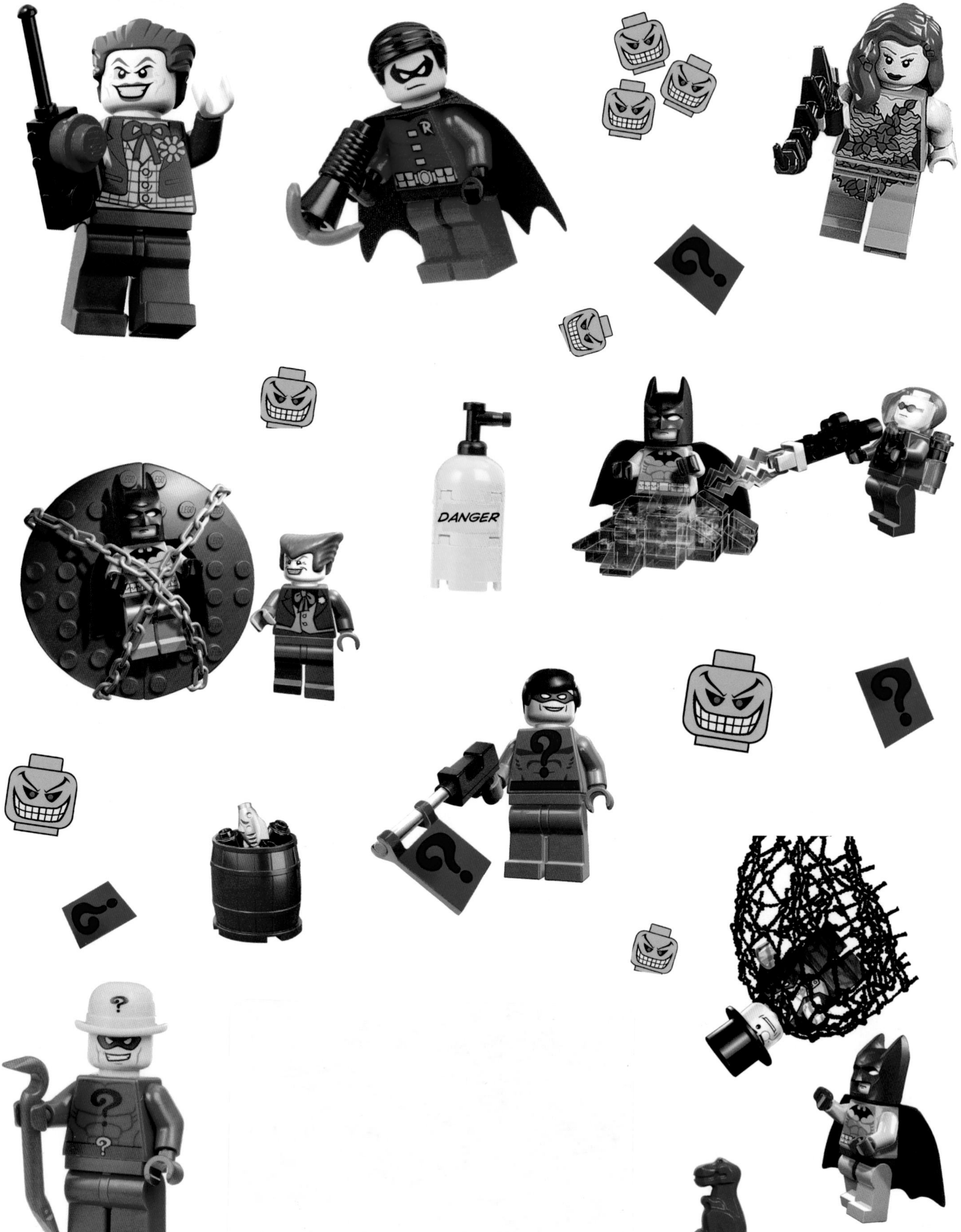
DANGER

EXTRA STICKERS

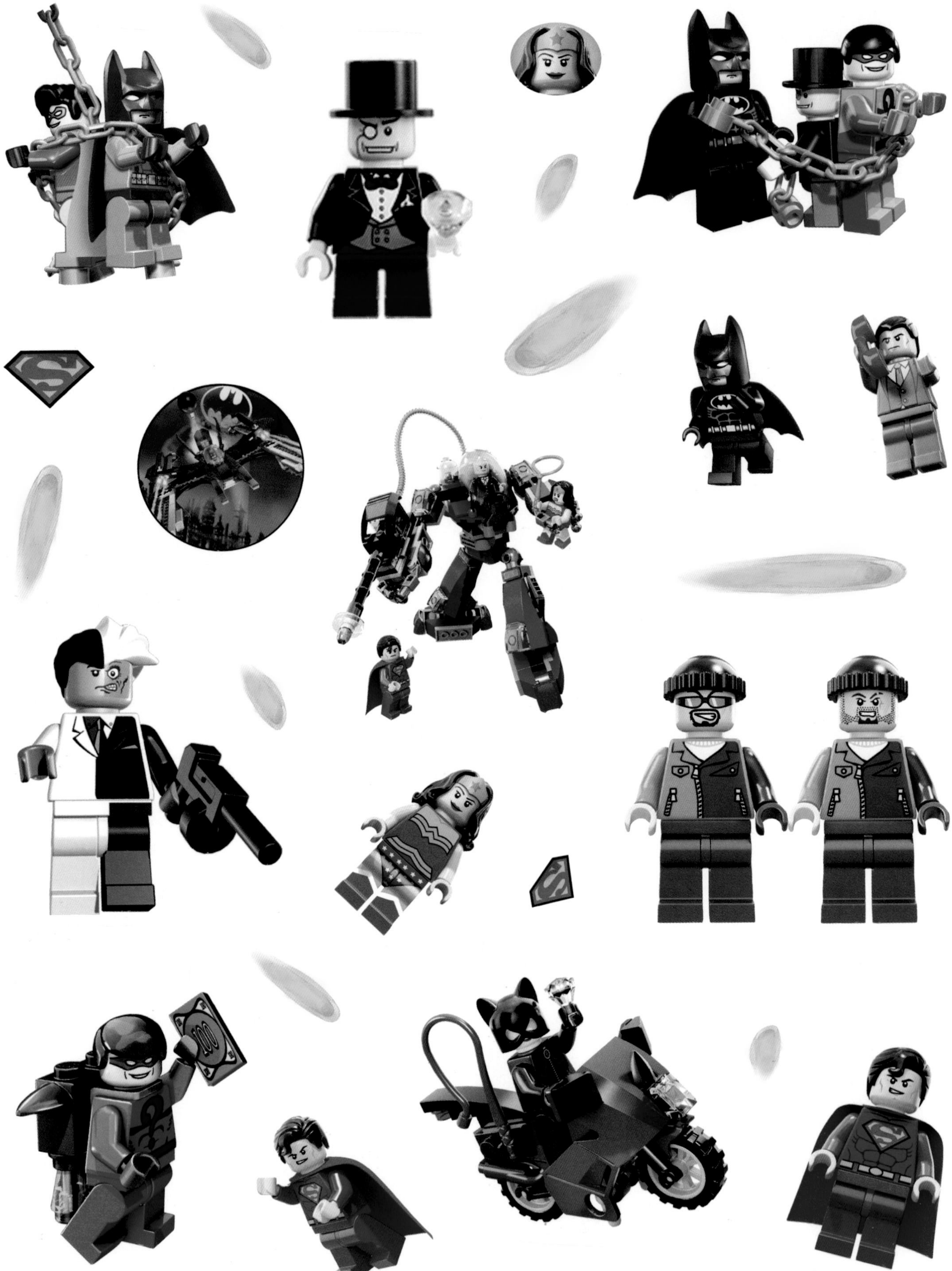
100

EXTRA STICKERS

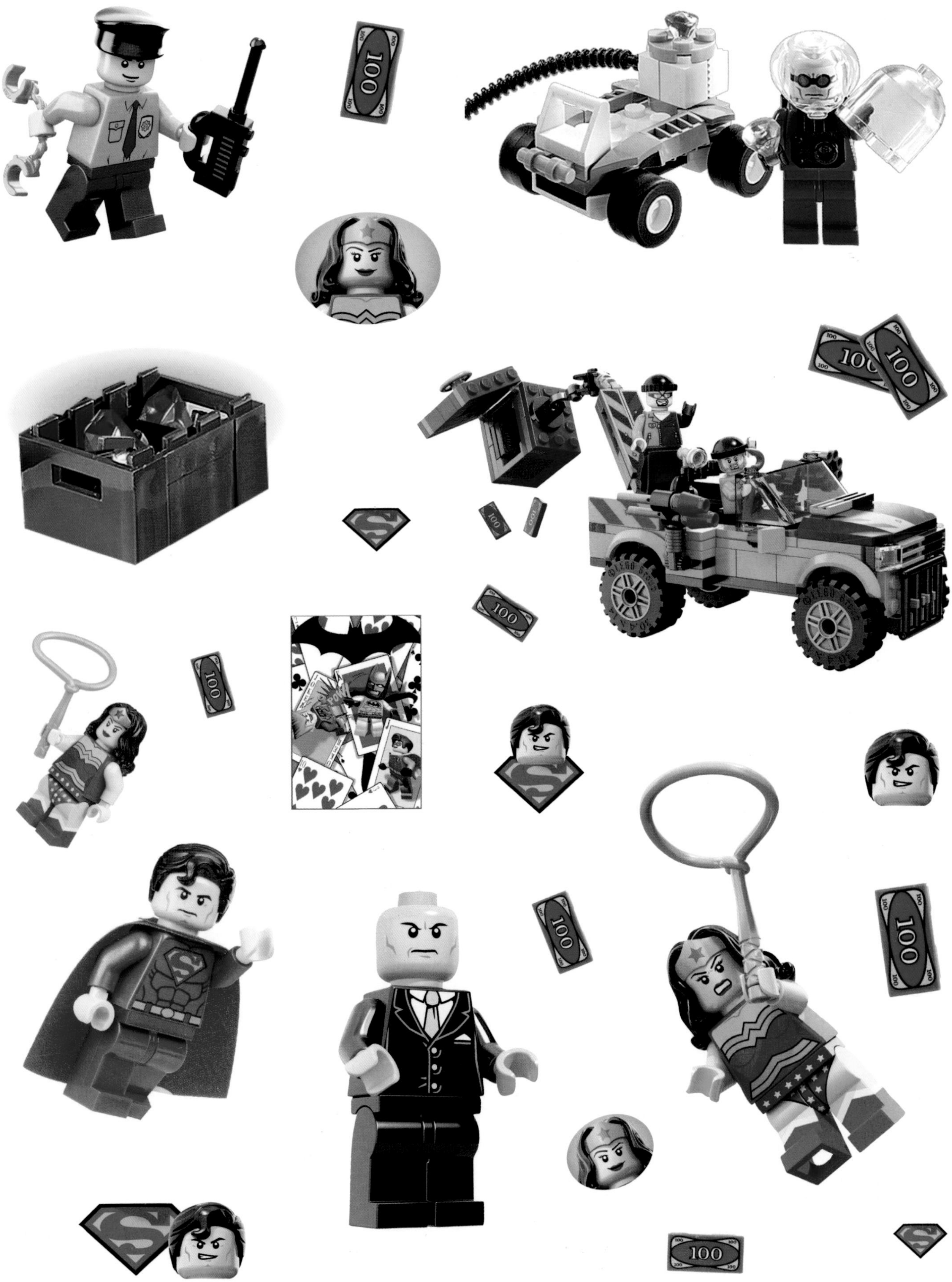

EXTRA STICKERS

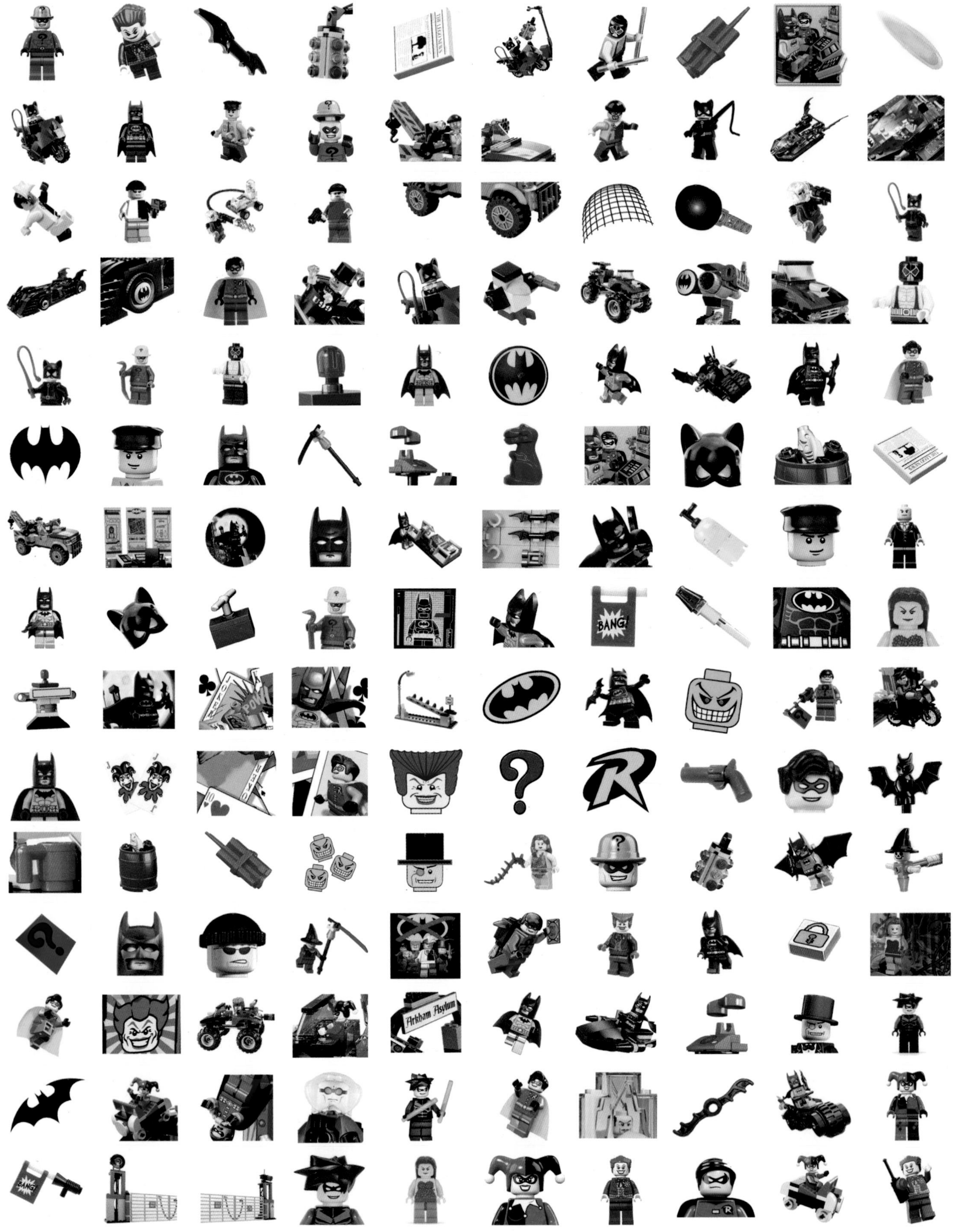
BANG!
Arkham Asylum

EXTRA STICKERS

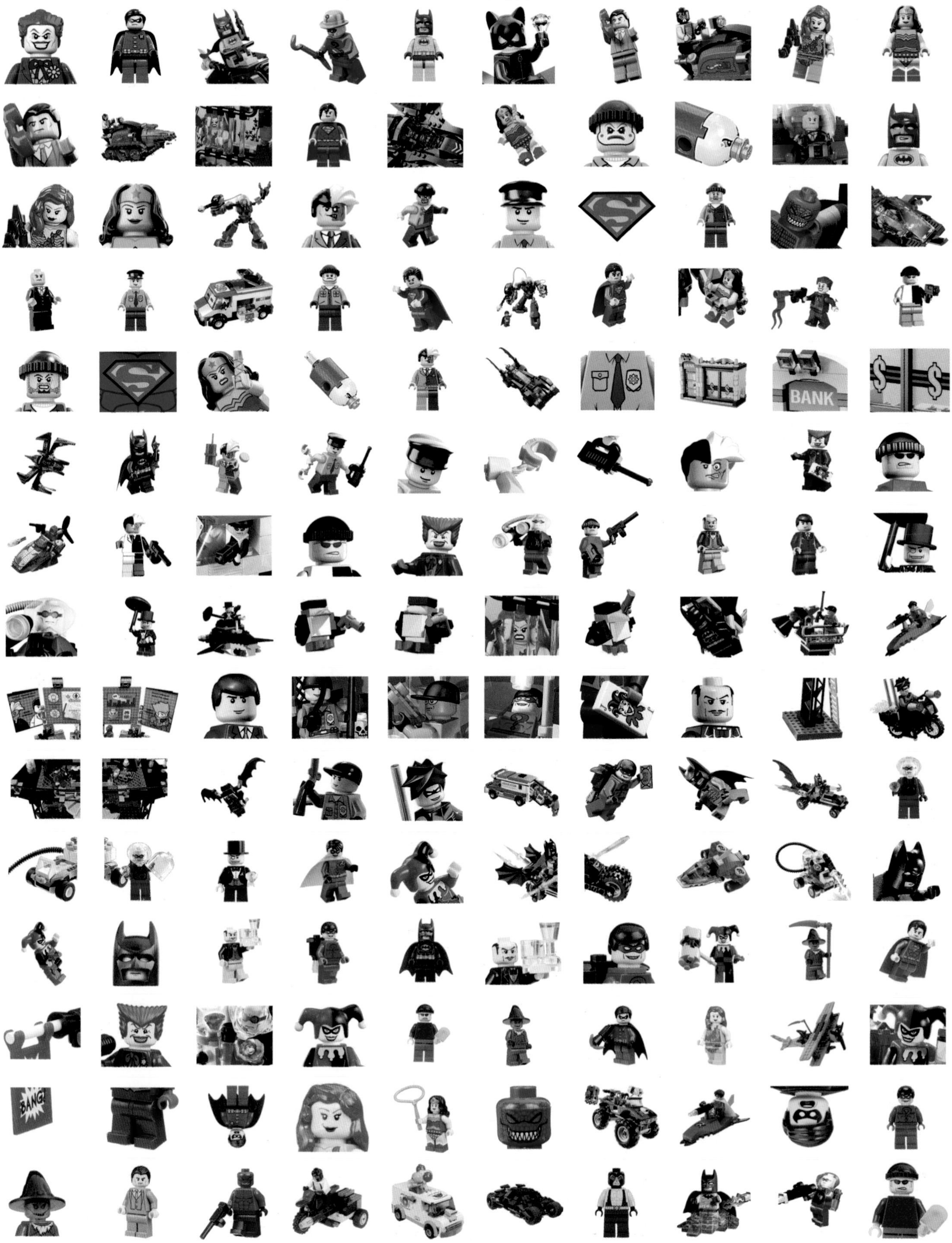
BANK
BANG!